Trouble at the Riding Camp

By Eli B. Toresen

Photos by Marielle Andersson Gueye
Translated by Osa K. Bondhus

Translator: Osa K. Bondhus
Repro: Bryne Offset A/S
Printed in Italy, 2007
Editor: Bobbie Chase

ISBN: 1-933343-67-2

Stabenfeldt, Inc.
457 North Main Street
Danbury, CT 06811
www.pony.us

Hi, PONY member!

I'm the kind of person who never wins anything... but would you believe it — this year
I actually won a contest for a riding camp!
At first I was overjoyed, but then reality hit
me — this would be the very first time I'd
stay somewhere on my own, surrounded by
total strangers! Even though I was allowed to
bring my pony, it felt kind of scary ... but I
knew I'd regret it forever if I chickened out, so
of course in the end I decided to go ...

On the following pages I'll tell you a little bit
about myself, and then you can read my
story... I'll tell you this right now — the
camp turned out to be far more eventful than
I'd ever imagined!

XXX
Shannon

Jo

PONY Member

This is me! (Shannon!!!)

Age: 13
Zodiac sign: Cancer
Favorite horse: Hero
(of course!!!)
Favorite horse breed:
Haflinger
Favorite food: Pizza
Worst food: Fish
Favorite color: Pink
Worst color: Beige

This is Hero!

Age: 10
Color: Chestnut with blaze
Favorite person: Me!!!
Favorite trick: Running back
to the stable (with me riding!)
Temperament: Nice, but can be
a bit stubborn
Favorite food: Carrots
Favorite gait: Canter
Likes: Cantering in the woods
Hates: Bulldozers

This is Haley!

Age: 19
Zodiac sign: Leo
Favorite horse: Lotus
Favorite horse breed:
Arab
Favorite food: Sushi
Worst food: Meatballs
Favorite color: Taupe
Worst color: Brown

This is Lotus!

Age: 8
Color: Gray
Favorite person: Haley
Favorite trick: Racing toward
obstacles
Temperament: High spirited,
needs an experienced rider
Favorite food: Oats
Favorite gait: Gallop
Likes: Jumping
Hates: Tractors

This is Vanessa!

Age: 13 1/2
Zodiac sign: Scorpio
Favorite horse: Balder
(and Hero)
Favorite horse breed:
Norwegian Fjord
Favorite food: Chinese
Worst food: Oatmeal
Favorite color: Blue
Worst color: Orange

This is Balder!

Age: 12
Color: Dun
Favorite person: Vanessa
Favorite trick: Keeping his
head up when Vanessa is going
to saddle him up.
Temperament: Calm and
reliable
Favorite food: Apples
Favorite gait: Walk
Likes: Eating
Hates: Goats

This is Chelsea!

Age: 13
Zodiac sign: Gemini
Favorite horse: Loki
Favorite horse breed:
Dutch Warmblood
Favorite food: Raspberries
Worst food: Fish
Favorite color: Red
Worst color: Beige

This is Loki!

Age: 11
Color: Bay
Favorite person: Chelsea
Favorite trick: Kicking when
he's gone over an obstacle
Temperament: Gentle, but can
be frisky
Favorite food: Carrots
Favorite gait: Gallop
Likes: Chasing the stable dogs
Hates: To stand still

This is Steven!

Age: We're not sure, but we think he must be ancient — probably at least 30.

Zodiac sign: Virgo

Favorite horse: He claims he loves all the horses equally (!)

Favorite horse breed: Trakehner

Favorite food: Steak

Worst food: Vegetables

Favorite color: Black

Worst color: Pink

Trouble at the Riding Camp

Chapter 1

Some Win, Some Lose

"I'm so excited I could die!" I cried. In my hand was an envelope bearing the logo of The Marlborough Riding Center. Would it be good news, or...? It had been quite a while since I submitted my answers to the contest, and I'd pretty much given up any hope of winning. I wasn't sure I even dared to check what the letter said.

"Mom! – You open it, please! I can't do it! What if it's bad news?"

Mom shook her head, laughing. "I don't think they'd even bother to send out letters to everybody who didn't win. But sure, I'll open it for you."

I held my breath and clenched my fists so hard the knuckles turned white. It would simply be too good to be true if I really was one of the few, lucky chosen who would get to spend two weeks with Haley Larson and her fantastic horse, Lotus.

When my best friend and I signed up for the contest I didn't really think there was much of a chance of winning. In fact, I hadn't even intended to enter at first. When I first saw the ad, I just skimmed it and tossed the magazine away.

"What's the point?" I said with a shrug. "I never win anything at all, and there must be hundreds of kids who are signing up."

"Honestly, Shannon!" Hannah lunged for the ad with fierce eagerness. "Why are you always so pessimistic? We have the same chance of winning as anybody else. C'mon, here's their web address. Let's sign up together, and then maybe we'll be selected together, too. Just imagine, a chance to go to a riding camp with Haley Larson, one of the world's best junior riders!"

So we signed up, answered a few questions about ourselves and how long we had been riding, plus some super easy questions about Haley Larson. At least they were easy for us, since we had been following her career ever since she participated in her first national eventing. And this letter might tell me that we had won,

or possibly that we hadn't. I watched mom impatiently as she used a pair of scissors to open the envelope. It seemed like she was moving in slow motion, and I felt a sudden urge to tear the letter out of her hands. But as long as I didn't know what it said, there was still a tiny hope... so I kept still and waited.

Mom unfolded the letter and started reading. "Hmmm," she said with a wrinkle between her eyes...

I could feel my heart sink. Her expression didn't look very promising.

Mom looked up and gazed at me. "Well, it seems as though I'll have to manage without your cheery face for a couple of weeks," she said.

At first I didn't comprehend what she was saying, but all of a sudden it was as if an army of butterflies started fluttering in my stomach. "Do you mean... that...?"

Mom nodded as her face broke into a

wide grin. "You and your horse have won a vacation at the riding camp! Congratulations, honey!"

I threw my arms around her neck and gave her a crushing hug, as if it was to her credit that I had won.

"This is the best thing that's ever happened to me, since you and Grandma bought Hero for me," I said, overjoyed. Hero had been my horse for two months now. He was a beautiful, kind, mixed breed pony, and I loved him more than anything in the world... well, except for my mom and grandmother, that is. I don't have a dad. He was killed in a car accident before I was born, so I only know him from pictures and home videos. But I have Mom and Grandma – one to raise me and one to spoil me, as Grandma always says. Neither of them have much money. They both work as teachers, and teachers don't exactly become millionaires (another quote by Grandma). Which is why I had not in my wildest dreams – well, actually, maybe only in my wildest dreams – imagined that I would someday own my own horse. I have loved horses since I was a little kid, and had been riding at the nearest riding school as often as possible. But own my own horse? That seemed like a pipe dream. How my mom and grandma had managed to keep it a secret was a mystery to me, because they usually run off at the mouth about anything and

everything. I know more about their colleagues than I ever wanted to know. But the purchase of this horse was one thing they had managed to keep totally quiet about. I'll never forget the shock of unsuspecting delight! Mom drove me to the riding school as usual that day, and I thought I was just going for another riding lesson. But when I arrived at the stable, Grandma was there, waiting for us in the farmyard. And next to her was a pony. The pony had a huge bow tied around his neck. And to the bow was attached a note which said that he was mine!

We keep Hero boarded at the riding school, in their boarding section for privately owned horses, and every time I walk in there I get all warm and fuzzy inside hearing the eager neighing with which he always greets me. I doubt that he and I will ever win any championships, but he is good at stadium jumping and we both enjoy it. I'd love to learn more and get better at it, but either way I'm more than content to just do it as a hobby. I have plenty of fun just admiring those who have great talent and ambition – like Haley Larson.

It was going to be totally fantastic, being around her for two whole weeks. I have seen lots of events and interviews with her on TV, and she seems like a very nice person.

"I'd better call Hannah," I said, dancing

across the floor. "We need to start making plans right away. The camp is only a week away!"

"But Shannon, you don't know if..." The rest of Mom's words were lost as I bounded up the stairs in order to get my cell phone, which I had left charging in my room.

It seemed like an eternity before Hannah answered.

"Hi," I said exuberantly. "Have you read the letter? Isn't this the most fantastic thing ever?"

"What letter? What are you talking about?"

"The letter from the riding camp – we won!"

"We didn't bring in the mail yet, so I haven't seen any letter." Hannah sounded baffled. "Are you serious? Did we actually win?"

"Well, that's kind of what I'm trying to tell you!" I was jumping up and down with impatience. "Run outside and get your letter, silly! And call me back when you've read it. We'd better start planning what to take!"

"I'm on it!" was the last thing I heard. Then a click told me that Hannah had hung up.

I sat down on the bed and waited for her to call me back. Happiness and excitement bubbled up inside me and made it impossible to sit still. Two weeks at this riding camp were going to be the best two weeks of my life!

Hannah sure was taking her time! I looked at my watch for the umpteenth time. It had been more than fifteen minutes since I talked to her. Was she so excited about the camp that she had completely forgotten about me? That wasn't like Hannah, though. Maybe she was on the phone with the center right now, asking if she could bring Pippi, the horse she takes care of. Hannah didn't actually own a horse, but since the guy who owns Pippi travels a lot she gets to ride her pretty much any time she wants. It was almost as good as having her own horse, but not quite.

After half an hour had passed since I talked to Hannah, I called her again.

"Weren't you going to call me back?" I said when she answered.

"There was nothing to call about," Hannah answered. She said it in a flat, unexcited tone of voice. "I didn't get any letter."

"You didn't? But... I thought..."

I fell silent, feeling confused. Then I quickly added, "Then you'll probably get it tomorrow. I'm sure you will! You know, we don't always get our Pony Club magazines on the same day either, so your letter is probably just a little delayed."

"Maybe so," said Hannah uncertainly. "But what if I didn't win?"

"Well, of course you did!" I tried to make my voice sound convincing, but felt a sudden pang of doubt. I had just assumed that since we signed up together, we would also be selected together, but that may not be how it worked.

"I hope you're right," mumbled Hannah. "It's not going to be easy having to wait for the mailman tomorrow!"

But Hannah didn't get any letter. One day passed... then two days... and at that point Hannah lost her patience and called the riding center. They didn't have good news for her.

"I wasn't selected," she said after she hung up, disappointed. "But you sure had some divine stroke of luck! You actually got in after an extra drawing that they did. They said something about having mistakenly selected two sisters. And according to the contest rules there can only be one winner from each family. Can you imagine how sad the girl who lost her place must have been?"

I could tell that Hannah was really sad too, but she was trying to be cool about it and be happy for me instead.

"I'm not so sure that I would have taken it as nicely as Hannah if she was the one who won and not me," I told my mom after I got back from the stable that evening.

"I think you would," said my mom. "I understand that you're sorry on Hannah's behalf, but you mustn't let that ruin the camp for you."

"But I can't go without Hannah!" I looked at Mom in astonishment. Suddenly it dawned on me, the full meaning of the fact that Hannah hadn't won. I would be going to a new place with a bunch of strangers! There was no way I would do that! The mere thought made me sick.

But Mom brushed aside my objections. "It's a great opportunity for you to have a vacation like this and get to spend time with a rider you've been admiring for such a long time. I'm sure you'll learn lots from her."

"How typical that you only think about me learning something," I mumbled, but at the same time I felt a pang of anticipation too. It was a fantastic opportunity, no doubt about that. But to go by myself, without Hannah...?

Mom seemed to read my mind, because she said, "It won't hurt you one bit to try to manage on your own for a little while, sweetheart. To tell you the truth, I've been thinking you seem a little too dependent on Hannah sometimes. And I'm sure you'll have a great time at this camp, not just an educational experience. Think about all the nice girls you'll meet – girls who have the same interests as you."

"How do you know they'll be nice?" I

asked stubbornly. "There are lots of girls at the stable who aren't very nice at all!"

After I got Hero, I had come to experience that fact firsthand, because of jealousy from some of the girls who didn't have their own horses. They had been nice enough before, but now suddenly they seemed to find fault with everything I did. If I hadn't had Hannah for support, I would have been a lot more upset about it.

What if it turned out like that at the riding camp? Who would be my supporter then? And suddenly the camp didn't seem very tempting to me anymore. I pictured myself standing all alone in a corner, while a group of girls – all of them older than I – whispered and laughed while they pointed at me. Nope, I was definitely not going!

I'll call the riding center right away and tell them I'm not coming. Then the whole problem will be over and done with, I thought, reaching for the phone.

Or... maybe I shouldn't call just yet. It was probably better to wait until morning anyway. But I was definitely going to call, that much was certain. Mom could say whatever she wanted. I was simply not brave enough to do this! And she wouldn't force me to do something I didn't want to do, would she?

Chapter 2

An Awkward Meeting

"Have a great time, sweetheart!" Mom was waving through the car window as she drove away with the horse trailer.

As I stood there watching the car leave I felt an increasing sense of panic. My hands had such a tight grip on the lead rope that they were getting all clammy. Hero remained calm and patient as he stood next to me and probably wondered what my problem was. This wasn't the first time we had gone somewhere together. He gave my arm a slight nudge with his muzzle, as if asking if I was going to stand around here all day. I took a deep breath and turned to the man who had waited silently while I said goodbye to my mom.

"So, Shannon – are you ready to check in?" He smiled as he reached out his hand toward me. "You can call me Steven. I'm the one who's in charge of the stable and the horses around here."

Steven had a good, firm handshake, and a friendly sparkle in his eyes. That helped me relax a little.

"What a nice pony you've got there, he said approvingly, and his words made me feel warm with happiness. If everyone here was as friendly as Steven, this may not turn out half bad after all.

I still had an unreal kind of feeling, like I couldn't quite grasp the fact that I was at a riding camp all by myself with a bunch of strangers, which was exactly what I had said I would not do. But I never got around to calling the center and canceling, maybe because some part of me still really wanted to go, even though I was scared stiff by the thought that I was being thrown into the deep end with no life preserver. In the end my mom had made the decision for me. "You simply cannot pass up a chance like this," she said. "If you do, you'll come to regret it, I'm sure of that!"

And I had a feeling she was right. If I didn't go, I would pass up probably the only chance in my life to meet my idol and maybe get to know her, learn from her...

Of course I would end up regretting it! But I may still not have done it, if Mom hadn't given me the choice of retreat.

"Why don't you give yourself three days?" she said. "If you still have a problem with it after three days, you can call me and I'll come and get you immediately."

"You promise?"

"Cross my heart and hope to die. But in return you have to promise me that you will really try to get to know the others before you decide whether you like it there or not. You can endure it for three days, can't you?"

Three days didn't sound nearly as bad as two weeks, so I agreed. After that I started looking forward to the camp, and dreading it at the same time. I have to admit that right before we left, though, I made a few extra trips to the bathroom. I was so nervous; my stomach was in complete turmoil.

But now that I was standing here with Steven it didn't seem quite so scary anymore. He seemed so nice and friendly, he would probably help me if I had any problems with the other kids, I thought optimistically.

Steven took me to the stable and showed me the stall where Hero would stay, and helped me put away the saddle and bridle in the saddle room.

"I will take care of feeding all of the horses," he said, giving Hero a carrot, which he chowed down happily – "but grooming and mucking out your particular horse's stalls is the responsibility of each camper."

"No problem," I said as I stroked Hero across his warm, soft muzzle. "I'd be happy to help out with the feeding too, if you need it. I do the same at the riding school back home, where I keep Hero boarded."

"That's nice of you." Steven smiled. "I'll let you know, you can count on it! But I think I hear another car outside. It's probably another camper arriving."

"Is everybody bringing their own horse?" I asked curiously.

Steven shook his head. "No, only four people are bringing their own horse. The other six campers will be riding ours. The center has twelve horses altogether. They're back toward the other end of the stable. This part is for our "visiting horses," as we call them.

Steven went into the hallway. "I'd better go and see who's here," he said. "You can stay here and enjoy a little time with your pony in the meantime, and then I'll come back in a little while and walk you over to the house so you can get your room and put your stuff away."

Steven left, and I felt my heartbeat quicken a little. Soon I would be meeting a new girl, or maybe a boy? I didn't know anything about the others who were coming to the camp. What if all the others were almost grown-up? What if I was the only thirteen-year-old, and all the others were much older than I? Then I would really feel like an outsider.

"Oh, come off it," I told myself, scratching Hero on the forehead. "There's no reason to cross any bridges before I get to them."

Hero gave a snort and rubbed his head against me. He seemed happy and relaxed. It didn't look like it bothered him to be in a strange place and a new stall. Of course

he had been moved only two months ago, so maybe he was getting used to dealing with new places. Mom and Grandma had found him at a riding center about thirty miles from the town where we live. The ad had appeared in the local paper.

"What a stroke of luck that they saw that particular ad and decided to get you," I said as I leaned into the nice warm body of the horse. My nervousness was going away – well, almost at least. No matter what the other kids were like, I had my wonderful pony. And three days would go quickly, so I probably didn't have anything to worry about... surely not...

"Hero! Is it really you? I didn't think I would ever see you again!" The voice startled me. I hadn't heard anybody coming into the stable, but there was Steven, with a girl who looked like she was about my age.

Before I had a chance to react, the girl came running, and opened the door to Hero's stall. Without paying any attention to me, she pushed herself past me and threw her arms around the neck of my pony.

"Oh, Hero, I've missed you so!" She buried her face in his mane. "I thought you were sold to a private person, not to a riding center! But here you are. I can't believe it!"

I stared at her in shock. Still with no acknowledgement of my presence, she lifted her head, stroked Hero across the muzzle and said to Steven, "You'll let me ride him while I'm here, won't you?"

"I'm sorry, Vanessa, but I'm afraid that's not possible." Apparently Steven was taken by surprise just as I was, and he looked like he didn't quite know how to handle this.

"Why not?" The girl, whose name apparently was Vanessa, looked at Steven, dumbfounded.

"Because I will be riding him," I said, noticing to my aggravation that my voice sounded high-pitched and shrill. "Hero is my horse."

Vanessa looked at me for the first time since she entered the stable. Now she looked at me up and down with narrow eyes. "Yours?"

I nodded. "Yes, I got him two months ago. Were you his groom?"

"Uh-huh..." Vanessa scratched Hero behind his ears. He lowered his head and looked like he enjoyed it. I felt a sudden pang of jealousy. But the next moment I felt ashamed. Was I that petty, that I couldn't handle the fact that Hero liked people other than just me?

There was a tense moment of silence. I didn't know what to say. Finally Steven broke the silence.

"Wow! It sure is a small world!" he said in an attempt to lighten the tension between us. "Imagine that, Hero's owner

and former groom meet right here at our stable. How's that for a funny coincidence, girls?"

Vanessa looked like she had bitten into something bitter, and the side-glance she gave me was anything but friendly.

"How long were you his groom?" I asked, just to say something.

"For two years! So I know him a lot better than you do! I had almost saved up enough money to buy him, when you came and snatched him away from me!"

Another hostile look. I didn't really understand why she reacted this way. Of course it must have been upsetting for her that she didn't get to buy Hero, but how was that my fault? I wasn't the one who had put him up for sale!

"I'm sure Shannon is happy to meet somebody who knows Hero so well," said Steven in another failed attempt to turn the mood. "It's always good to learn as much as possible about a horse you've bought. I bet the two of you will become fast friends and have a lot to talk about."

Right! I thought, while Vanessa turned her back to me and started stroking and cuddling Hero, as if it was her pony and I didn't exist.

Steven shrugged his shoulders, looking a little resigned. "Well, let's go up to the house," he said. "You can check out your rooms and bring in your luggage. After lunch there'll be an informative meeting and possibly a short ride."

Vanessa squeezed past me, jabbing her elbows into my ribs as she did, hard enough to make me groan in pain, but Steven didn't notice what she did, and I didn't say anything.

If the other campers were as unfriendly as Vanessa, it was sure going to be three "delightful" days before I could call Mom and ask her to come and get me, I thought gloomily while I trudged along after Steven and Vanessa over to the house. All I needed now was to find out that Vanessa and I would be sharing a room!

"If we are, I swear I'll take Hero and run away!" I mumbled to myself. Not on my life was I going to be roommates with that hateful girl, who acted like she owned my pony.

When we arrived at the house, we were greeted by a friendly lady who gave us a big smile and introduced herself as Brenda. She told us she was in charge of the food and other housekeeping matters.

"But I'm not going to clean up your rooms or make your beds, just so you know," she said. "You'll have to tidy up your own rooms, but do let me know if you need more towels or soap or that kind of stuff. We live a simple and practical life as much as possible around here. But you'll figure that out for yourselves."

Brenda walked upstairs with us. Fortunately, it turned out that we were all going to stay in single rooms. Vanessa and I each got a room at opposite ends of a long hallway that had several rooms on each side. I wasn't sorry about that. The more distance between us the better. I had a bad feeling that Vanessa was going to mean trouble, if not for Hero then at least for me...

Chapter 3

Sneaky and Jealous

"Good job, everybody! Let's take a break for an hour." Steven was standing by the fence to the arena and waved invitingly with some bottles of soda.

I leaned forward and patted Hero's neck. "You did really well today," I praised him.

For the first time since I came to the camp, I felt relaxed and happy. And I didn't need to look around to know the reason. Vanessa wasn't at the riding lesson this morning. She had a migraine and was staying in bed. I guess I should feel sorry for her, but all I could feel was a great relief. Today I was able to concentrate on what I was doing, without being worried about sarcastic remarks from her. She was very good at covering them up as helpful advice, and at least Steven had fallen for her act. He seemed to think that I ought to fall to my knees in gratitude to Vanessa for helping me so much. And as long as Steven was nearby, Vanessa acted like the perfect, benevolent soul who was helping me get to know my pony better.

But as soon as she had me to herself, she used every opportunity to dish out mean and malicious comments that were breaking down whatever little self-confidence I had. And there was nothing I could do about it. If I were to complain to Steven, he would just think I was being ungrateful and difficult. As far as he was concerned, Vanessa was clearly without fault.

I slid down from Hero's back and led him out of the training arena. No point in thinking about Vanessa right now, though. That would just destroy my great mood. I stroked Hero across the ridge of his nose and was instantly filled with joy that this beautiful, kind pony really was mine.

And I didn't need to stay here if I didn't want to. Tomorrow would be my third day at the camp, and that's how long I had promised my mom to stick it out. One phone call, and she would come and get me. And then I wouldn't have to worry about Vanessa ever again! Except... What

if she regarded it as a victory that she'd gotten rid of me? I hadn't thought about it that way...

"Hey, are you asleep? Here, take this!"

I startled, then turned around and gratefully accepted the soda that Chelsea was offering me. Even though she and Vanessa were the only campers that were my own age, I hadn't talked to her very much yet. But she seemed like a nice girl.

I grabbed the bottle and opened it. It was nice and cold. Wonderful! I took a deep swallow and smiled at Chelsea.

"Thank you! I was just standing here thinking about how lucky I am to get to come to this camp," I lied. "Actually I wasn't even among the initial winners, but was selected in an extra drawing."

"That was you?" Chelsea stared at me.

"Yes, I could hardly believe it," I said. "But how did you know...?"

I fell silent as it occurred to me. "Was it your sister who lost her place?"

Chelsea nodded. "Steven left it up to my parents to decide which one of us should get to come. My dad thought we should share and go for one week each, but my sister refused and demanded that we draw straws on it. It's not easy to say no to Courtney; she can be incredibly bossy sometimes. So I accepted, even though I knew she would win, because she always has before."

Chelsea shrugged her shoulders.

"However, this time I was the winner. Courtney got really mad, and wanted us to share the vacation after all. But my mom put her foot down and told Courtney that she was the one who had insisted on drawing over it. Besides, I think Mom also thought that it would be good for me to get away for a couple of weeks and learn to manage on my own."

"Exactly what my mom said too! I didn't want to go without my best friend, but my mom talked me into it."

"Well, then we're kind of in the same boat, aren't we?" For a moment it looked like Chelsea was thinking about something unpleasant, but then her face lit up. "I'm glad you didn't chicken out. You and that Vanessa girl are the only ones here who are my age."

The way she referred to Vanessa indicated that she didn't like her much. Maybe it was just wishful thinking on my part, but I started nurturing the notion that if Chelsea and I became friends, it would be easier to cope with Vanessa.

"Look at that!" Chelsea exclaimed before I had a chance to say any more. "Apparently Haley is going to practice while we're on a break. She just rode into the arena. How about we put our horses in the pasture and go watch her?"

Chelsea was already heading toward the enclosure behind the stable. I gathered up Hero's reins and followed her.

"Let's just leave the saddles and bridles right here," suggested Chelsea while she loosened the girth and started pulling the saddle off of the horse she was borrowing. I realized I didn't know its name so I asked her.

"Loki," said Chelsea. "Apparently all of the horses at this stable have Old Norse names – you know, from Norse mythology?"

"You're right!" I said. "I hadn't thought about that before you said it."

I knew that the horse Vanessa was riding was called Balder, and I seemed to remember that Steven had called one of them Odin. But that was all I knew. I had no idea what the other horses were named, and I didn't remember the names of very many of the campers either, even though we had been riding together for two days now. I suddenly realized that I had been so preoccupied with Vanessa that everything else had become secondary. Why was I allowing that mean girl to dominate my thoughts like this?

I put Hero's saddle on the ground. Then I undid the straps of the bridle, opened the gate and gave my pony a friendly push behind. He didn't need much persuading. Eagerly he jumped onto the inviting, green grass, only too happy to be rid of

the saddle. He lay down, rolling around contentedly before he got back up and started munching on grass as if he hadn't been fed for days. I smiled as I looked at him. There could be no doubt that he liked it here. So why had I refused to let myself do the same? Vanessa was unpleasant, no doubt about that, but was that really my problem? Only if I continued to let it be, it suddenly dawned on me.

"Are you coming?" Chelsea's voice interrupted my thoughts.

"Sure," I said absentmindedly as I followed her. I threw one last glance at Hero. My mind was still focused on Vanessa and

me. What if I were to turn the tables on her? Until now I had let it shine through that it kind of bothered me, the fact that she knew so much about my pony. And it was clear that she, on her part, enjoyed my lack of confidence.

How would she react if I started pretending to be happy to hear all of her "helpful advice"? That would make her lose her power over me...

"... And maybe she'll see that she needs to give it up," I thought out loud.

"Did you say something?" Chelsea turned toward me.

"Uh... I just said I look forward to watching Haley and Lotus training."

I smiled at Chelsea and decided that from now on I would ignore Vanessa as much as I could, and instead try to get to know Chelsea. She seemed really nice, and probably so were the others, even if they were older than we were. So what if Vanessa carried on with her silly comments? I wasn't going to pay any attention to them any more. I'd show her!

A little later I felt my mood soaring as I stood by the arena and watched Haley and Lotus jump one hurdle after another with hardly any effort. Every now and then it almost looked like Lotus had invisible wings, flying high above the hurdles.

"That horse should've been named Pegasus, and not Lotus," said Chelsea, as if she had read my mind.

I nodded. "Imagine, being able to jump like that!" I said enviously. "Haley makes it look so simple, as if she and the horse are one, in a way."

"Uh-huh... it's just like with my brother," said Chelsea. "I mean, he doesn't ride, but he plays the piano. And when he plays, it looks so incredibly easy and effortless. But he also practices for several hours each day to be that good, so talent isn't all there is to it. You have to work hard at it if you want to be really good at something."

"I think I'll pass," I said with a shudder. "I'm totally fine with practicing two to three times a week, but several hours every day? No thank you! I'd rather go for a ride with Hero and just have fun."

"Same here!" Chelsea nodded. "Horses are supposed to be fun, not just a lot of work. Though, I must say, it really does look wonderful when someone can ride really well, like Haley."

We hung around by the arena until Haley was done training. When she left, she waved to us, but she didn't stop to chat.

"Do you think Haley will come to our lesson this time?" I looked at Chelsea.

She shrugged her shoulders. "I doubt it. Steven hasn't said anything. To be honest, I thought she was going to be more involved with us."

"Me too! After all, that was the impres-

sion they gave in the brochure for the contest. But so far we've barely even had a chance to talk to her."

Maybe I was naive, but I had actually thought that Haley was going to be with us the whole time, riding with us, talking to us, just like any other kid at the camp. But that wasn't how it had turned out. Haley kept to herself, trained by herself, and only spent a short period of time with us each day. I had no idea where she had her meals. Not with us, at least. Yesterday she had joined our riding lesson for about 15 minutes, and then she disappeared. I saw her ride toward the woods, and felt a pang of envy. It would have been so great to ride with her. But apparently she felt she was above the rest of us. I hadn't really expected that. But of course she was a star, or at least a budding star, and maybe this was how stars behave. I don't know, but I have to admit I was a little disappointed.

"Of course it's great to get to watch her train," said Chelsea. "And Steven said that Haley is going to teach us some jumping, so I guess we'll just have to wait and see when 'her highness' steps down to our level."

I had to laugh. "She can glide along up there as long as she wants to," I said.

"Let's go and get our horses, and see what happens next. It'll probably be fun regardless. Steven is good too."

"And tomorrow we're going for a trail ride, and we may even have a barbecue", said Chelsea. "I'm looking forward to that!"

And to my surprise I noticed that I was looking forward to it as well. Now that I had made friends with Chelsea, it was totally out of the question to call Mom and ask her to come and get me. I was not alone anymore, and I was determined to show that I could handle Vanessa.

My high, bravado-laced spirits lasted all the way to the pasture. Hero was there, just as I had expected him to be. But what I had not expected was that someone was sitting on his back. Or rather, someone was practically lying on his back.

Vanessa! The sight hit me like a fist in the stomach. I thought she was still in bed sick, but here she was with my pony, looking like she owned both him and the rest of the world. In one second flat my sensible plan about beating her at her own game was all but forgotten. How dared she?

Vanessa leaned on Hero's back with one hand, while lazily scratching my pony's mane with the other. And Hero, that unfaithful horse, looked like he relished it completely. For a moment I was so angry I was fuming. Enough already!

Vanessa's triumphant smile as I marched toward her, ready to tell her off,

showed with unmistakable clarity that she had done this on purpose to tease me.

All the furious words which were bubbling up inside me were almost spilling out, when it suddenly occurred to me that this was exactly what she was after – for me to lose my temper in front of my new-found friend. Then Vanessa would act graceful and hurt and taken by surprise, and everyone would feel soooo sorry for her. Not only had her favorite horse been sold right out from under her nose, but here I was, the petty new owner, who wouldn't even allow her a few precious minutes with this pony. I would become "that meanie, Shannon" for the rest of the camp, while Vanessa would bask in the glory of being seen as the brave girl who handled adversity with a heroic smile.

All of this passed through my mind in a matter of seconds, and I shut my mouth so hard the pain shot from my teeth to the roots of my hair. For a moment I envisioned a horrific scene of crushed teeth falling out of my mouth if I opened it again. But the unpleasant feeling subsided and I realized that my teeth were just fine. Then I took a deep breath and, with tight fists, I looked Vanessa straight in the eye. My smile felt stiff and not very genuine, but I held on to it while saying in as friendly a manner as possible when you would rather throw someone to the

ground, "Well, this is a nice surprise, I thought you were sick."

The malicious smirk on Vanessa's face disappeared. All of a sudden she looked bewildered. This was definitely not the reaction she had been expecting.

"It helped to have a little nap. I feel fine now. Fortunately my migraines don't usually last very long."

"And you're so thoughtful to keep Hero company while Chelsea and I were watching Haley. That was very nice of you. I'm grateful."

If it's true that lightning strikes those who lie, then I'm sure in big trouble now! I thought, glancing up at the sky.

Vanessa looked totally shocked. "You mean, you don't mind?" she blurted out.

"Oh, no! Why should I?" I shrugged my shoulders and put on a face of innocence. "You know Hero better than I do, as you've said yourself. After all, you were his groom, and it's natural for you to miss him. You go ahead and cuddle him as much as you want when I'm not riding him. He loves to be petted."

Vanessa looked as if she'd just eaten a bug. She glared at me, but found no way out of the trap that she had made for herself. Clearly she had expected me to yell and scream and make a total fool of myself. Instead I had done the opposite, and she had no idea how to handle it.

"Hey, we'd better get our horses ready for the lesson." Chelsea broke the tense moment.

Vanessa quickly got down from Hero's back. "Balder is in the stable, so I have to go and get him now," she said without looking at me.

I couldn't help gloating a little as I watched her go. I had handled that one quite well, I thought. I felt sure that Vanessa would think twice about trying to mess with me again. Finally I had proven to myself that I could deal with her. And when she saw that I wasn't going to be ruffled no matter how much she coddled Hero, she would probably get tired of it soon and leave me alone.

I was suddenly convinced that the rest of this vacation was going to be super. Little did I know, while I contentedly tightened the girth around my pony's tummy, that the trouble I had seen so far was nothing compared to the troubles ahead...

Chapter 4

The Night Riders

"My arms are aching after all that training, but it sure was a lot of fun!"

I sighed happily as I took a swallow from a mug of hot chocolate. It had been a beautiful day, but the temperature had suddenly dropped, and it was getting chilly outside. Which meant it was a perfect evening for some indoor fun.

Chelsea nodded. "I really learned a lot from Haley today. Man, that girl is good!"

To our surprise and delight, Haley not only instructed us in jumping, she also joined us for dinner. Right now she was sitting in the living room talking to Steven, and it looked as if she was having a good time, just like the rest of us.

Hannah would have been really jealous if she saw me right now, I thought, and felt a pang of guilty conscience. Hannah! I hadn't thought about her once until this moment, even though I had promised to send her tons of text messages and tell her how everything was. Okay, when I promised that, I didn't know that we wouldn't be allowed to use cell phones at our riding lessons or in the common rooms. But still... there had been plenty of opportunities to send messages at other times.

"I'm gonna run upstairs and get a sweater," said Chelsea, and she got up. "I'm cold."

"Mm-mm," I mumbled distractedly. My mind was still on Hannah.

If she had been the one who was here, and I was sitting back home not hearing anything from her, I would have been hopping mad by now. I'd better call her tonight as soon as I get to my room and try to make it up to her... I would...

A nudge in the shoulder made me jump and almost spill my hot cocoa. I looked up. Vanessa was leaning over me with a big smile on her face. But it didn't take me long to realize that the smile was for the others in the room, because the look in her eyes gave me chills.

"You think you can brush me off by pretending to be generous and wanting to share Hero with me?" she said in a voice so quiet that nobody else could hear it. "How stupid do you think I am?"

"What... what do you mean?" I looked at her, shocked, and felt my newfound self-confidence trickle away. The expression in her eyes scared me.

"Hero should have been mine! And you know it! You had no right to buy my favorite pony. I've missed him so much it hurts, but I'm sure that doesn't mean anything to a spoiled brat who gets everything she wants! It must be easy when you can just see a horse one day and decide that you want him on a whim."

"But I... I... it wasn't me who..." My words fell on deaf ears. Vanessa had turned her back on me. She strode over to a chair across the room. From there she continued to glare at me with narrow, peering eyes. It was a very unpleasant feeling. And why was Chelsea taking so long? It felt as if she had been gone for an eternity. She said she was getting a sweater, not knitting one! I tried to ignore Vanessa while I watched the door. If Chelsea didn't show up soon, maybe I should go up to my room and call Hannah.

Seconds and minutes ticked away while I felt Vanessa's eyes burn into my neck. I couldn't stand this any longer! Just as I was about to get up, Chelsea finally appeared. She dropped down on the chair beside me with a dejected and almost bitter expression on her face. Clearly something had happened.

"I almost gave up on you," I said. "I was starting to wonder if you had been kidnapped or something."

"Sorry! It was Courtney. She... she called just as I got up to my room. We argued... She's so stubborn!"

Chelsea made a face. "Ugh, but let's not talk about my stupid sister. I don't even want to think about her. But speaking of arguing... What's up with you and Vanessa?"

"Oh, we don't exactly argue," I said reluctantly, not feeling sure if I should confide in Chelsea. What if she didn't believe me? I did have the impression that she didn't like Vanessa too much, but that could just have been my imagination. Toward everyone else, Vanessa acted totally nice and friendly. It wasn't difficult to see that the others at the riding camp liked her just fine. I would probably have liked her too, if she had given me a chance.

"If you're not arguing, then what is going on between you?" Chelsea looked at me.

"It wasn't really much of anything, only a silly misunderstanding." I shrugged my shoulders. "She wanted to buy Hero and thinks that I snatched him away from her. But that's not how it was..."

Chelsea seemed curious to find out more, but just then Steven clapped his hands and said, "Not only are we so lucky that we get to use Haley in our riding lessons,

but tonight we will also get to enjoy another one of her talents. The floor is yours, Haley!"

Haley got up, smiling. "I wouldn't exactly call it a talent, but I love telling stories. And in particular –" she made her voice low and mysterious "– in particular, I love ghost stories..."

I would have liked to get up and say, "Please don't, please tell something else instead," but I didn't, of course. Besides, any pitiful little protest coming from me would have been drowned out by the others'

delighted cheers, anyway. I've always been terribly afraid of the dark and shied away from scary stories, at least just before bedtime. But now I stayed where I was. I didn't want the others to find out that I was scared of a ghost story. Nobody likes to advertise, "look at me, what a chicken I am," right? So I didn't get up and leave, even though Haley's words gave me goose bumps. And that was before she'd even started her story.

"What I'm about to tell you is said to be a true story," she said. "It is a spine-chilling story that requires dimmed lights…"

A moment later, we were sitting in a semi-dark room, which didn't help one bit! I curled up in my chair and wondered if anyone would notice if I held my hands over my ears. At the same time I was a little curious too about what Haley was about to tell us, so naturally I ended up keeping my hands away from my ears, even though I knew inside that I would regret it later.

"Once upon a time, a long time ago, there was a small farm by the edge of the woods here, in the meadow right behind the stable…" Haley's voice had a dark, almost hypnotic ring to it, and I knew what Steven had meant when he said she was a talented storyteller. It was impossible not to listen to her…

"It was in that meadow they were first seen – two mysterious figures which eventually became known as "The Night Riders…""

I was lying in my bed, shivering from head to toe. Not because it was cold, but because I was scared. How I wished I had acted on my first instinct and gone to bed before Haley told her story! Then I might have been able to sleep now, instead of lying here imagining that I heard all kinds of strange sounds inside as well as outside.

Every attempt at forcing my thoughts over to something more pleasant – like my pony, for example – ended with me picturing a frightening sight of the Night Riders Haley had told us about. I had seen them vividly with my inner eye while she told the story. Two merciless, mysterious figures that rode through the dark of night looking for children.

As soon as I closed my eyes, I could hear Haley's voice inside my head. "To this day nobody knows if it was people or ghosts who haunted this town… but every time they showed up, a small child disappeared, never to be seen again…"

Haley did say that nobody had seen the Night Riders in more than fifty years, but what if they were still out there? What if they were watching this house right now? A house filled with kids… not that we were a bunch of small children, but still… A drawn-out, scraping sound startled me. What was that? Did the sound come from the hallway or outside? And that shadow in the corner of my room… was that just a chair? Didn't it look more like a person crouching down? Had somebody snuck in here while I was sitting in the living room? Hidden in the closet?

My heart was beating hard and fast, and my mouth felt dry. I sat up in bed and turned on the night lamp. The bright light stung my eyes, but anything was better than lying here in the dark,

surrounded by strange, scary noises and shadows...

I lay down again, trying to relax. When I pulled the comforter halfway over my head, the light didn't bother me as much. And as long as there was light, I was safe... My head felt warm and light... and

I slowly fell into an uneasy sleep, dreaming that I was searching for a hiding place where the Night Riders wouldn't find me. And it was urgent, because I could hear the hoof beats... Soon they would be here...

When I woke up the next morning, all the scary shadows were gone. In bright sunlight it was hard to understand how I could have been so scared the night before. After all, it was just an old fairy-tale – most likely invented by somebody who wanted to scare their children into obedience – otherwise The Night Riders would come and get them...

Grandma once told me that when she was little, she was told that she must never go to the pond in the woods, because if she did, Little Champ would get her. Little Champ was supposedly a smaller relative of the famous Lake Champlain monster, and it lived in the pond. It wasn't until she was grown up that she finally realized that this was just something her parents had scared her with in order to keep her from going to the pond and possibly falling in and drowning...

You'd think it would have been a lot simpler to tell the truth, but regardless, it had worked. Grandma had kept away from the pond. And this was probably the same kind of story. Why had I not realized that last night?

I hurried into the bathroom, embarrassed at myself for being so ridiculously scared of the dark. It was time for me to outgrow such fears! Because I didn't really believe in ghosts, did I...?

No, of course I didn't! I made a face at myself in the mirror and wished I were more like Hannah. She would have just laughed at Haley's story and found it amusing.

Hannah! I had forgotten her again! First I was so caught up in Vanessa and my problems with her that I totally forgot about my best friend! And now I had done it again because of some stupid ghost story! What was wrong with me?

I ran back to my room and got out my cell phone. I felt terrible when I saw the text message from Hannah: "Silence is not golden! Are you alive or not?"

"Sorry! My cell phone died! Okay now. Wish you were here! Call you tonight, Shannon."

The thing about my cell phone being dead wasn't true, but I didn't want Hannah to be mad at me, so a little white lie seemed like a good idea. Quite pleased with myself, and totally determined to keep my promise to Hannah about calling later, I went to the bathroom to get ready for the ride. I was both looking forward to it and dreading it, but was determined about one thing: I was not going to let Vanessa catch me off guard again! I would show her that I wasn't scared off by her behavior. What exactly could she do to me anyway? Hero was mine, and she was going to have to come to terms with that. For a moment I felt an annoying feeling of pity for her, because I couldn't help thinking how I would have felt if somebody

had taken Hero away from me. The mere thought of it made my stomach tighten, but at the same time I knew that I didn't have any reason to feel guilty. Vanessa's behavior was silly and completely unfair. She should be angry at the people who sold Hero, if she absolutely had to, but not at me.

"Maybe I should tell Chelsea the whole story," I said to my own mirror image. "She seems nice, and it would be great to have somebody on my side if Vanessa starts getting totally unbearable."

The idea seemed fine at the time. After one last glance in the mirror I put away the hairbrush. Then I went downstairs to eat breakfast, blissfully ignorant of the horrible surprise that was waiting for me.

Chapter 5

Going For a Ride, Taking Things In Stride

"Hey! Wait for me!" Haley's voice pulled me out of the gloomy thoughts that were about to destroy my day.

I pulled up on Hero as I threw a glance over my shoulder. Haley was galloping toward me. Lotus was as elegant as ever. The tall, strong horse galloped so lightly and effortlessly it looked like she floated along the trail. The sight made me think about what Chelsea had said, about Pegasus being a more fitting name. Chelsea – it stung as I thought about what had happened when I came down for breakfast. I had thought that Chelsea was nice and fun, and that she liked me...

"What's the matter? You look as if you've found you've been backing the wrong horse," said Haley gently when she pulled up on Lotus next to me.

I blinked and was shocked to realize that I was on the verge of tears. I tried frantically to force them back. The last thing I needed now was to act like a cry-baby in front of my idol!

But I couldn't stop them. Two big tears were trickling down my cheeks. Quickly I wiped them away, but I wasn't quick enough. Haley had seen them and asked with concern, "Why are you riding all by yourself? Is something wrong? Did something happen?"

I shook my head. "No, it's nothing really, I'm just being stupid... and I'm not alone, not really. The others aren't that far ahead, I just..."

I fell silent, not sure what to say. A part of me felt like opening up and telling Haley all about my worries, because maybe she could help me. But it was too embarrassing. I couldn't tell her that I was sad because Chelsea had betrayed me for Vanessa, just as I thought I had found a friend here...

I don't know what Haley was able to tell from my face, but suddenly she said, "Wait here! I just need to say something to Steven real quick!"

She drove Lotus into motion, and as I

watched, the elegant equipage disappeared rapidly down the trail. Haley emanated such effortless self-confidence that I noticed another lump in my throat. If only I could be as self-confident as she was. Haley would probably have just shrugged her shoulders arrogantly at Vanessa and Chelsea, making them feel like losers.

I held tightly onto Hero's reins, prepared for him to try to follow after Lotus, but he just lowered his head and seemed more interested in checking out the grass on the side of the trail. This was completely unlike him. Normally Hero gets all riled up if he thinks there is going to be a gallop. There's nothing better to him than getting to stretch out on a nice riding trail. I felt a sudden pang of fear. Was he getting sick or something? But it didn't look like he was hurting anywhere. And there was certainly nothing wrong with his appetite. He had a mouth full of grass, which he eagerly chowed down. Maybe yesterday's training had tired him out. I told myself that must be it, even though I knew deep down that we hadn't really trained that hard. I patted Hero absent-mindedly on the neck and closed my eyes. Right now my mind was more centered on my problems with Vanessa and Chelsea, anyway. The scene from this morning kept coming back to me...

I had been in high spirits when I went down for breakfast, but my good mood sank considerably the moment I caught sight of Chelsea. We had agreed to eat together, but now she was sitting next to Vanessa. They were chatting and laughing, and looking as if they were the best friends in the world. I wasn't sure what to do – go over to Chelsea and say hi, or pretend that I hadn't seen her and sit down somewhere else?

Vanessa made the decision for me. She gave me an icy cold look, then leaned toward Chelsea and whispered something to her. Chelsea giggled and glanced over at me. You didn't need the IQ of a genius to comprehend that it was me they were talking about. I felt my head getting warm. Yesterday it had definitely looked like Chelsea was more interested in being with me than with Vanessa. So what had happened? Vanessa must have said something that made her change her mind. I wondered what she had said, but couldn't very well ask.

I gave the two of them a smile, which I hoped looked self-assured, before seating myself as far away from them as possible. Brenda was serving up a bunch of yummy food that would normally have made my mouth water, but now I had completely lost my appetite. I forced down a piece of toast with some jam.

And as I sat there chewing my food – which might as well have been cardboard

due to my current lack of interest in it – I tried to make a plan. When we got out to the stable, I would try to pull Chelsea aside and ask her what was going on. I regretted now that I hadn't told her about Vanessa's jealousy last night. But today I would. If I just got a chance to talk to her we'd be friends again, and Chelsea would understand that Vanessa was being jealous and malicious.

I got the chance when Vanessa left to go and get her grooming tools. As my hands got clammy with nervousness, I hurried over to Chelsea.

"I thought we'd agreed to have breakfast together," I said as I looked at her. "So why did you sit with Vanessa?"

Chelsea shrugged her shoulders. "I can sit with whomever I choose, can't I?" She turned her back to me and walked toward Loki's stall.

I looked at her go. Tears of anger and

frustration welled up in my eyes, and I got a lump in my throat. Clearly Vanessa had managed to make her switch sides. She'd probably never believe me now, no matter what I said to her. What had I done to deserve this?

I walked wearily toward Hero's stall. "If you're going to groom Loki, I'll be happy to help you!" I heard Vanessa say behind me.

"That's very nice of you," said Chelsea, "but don't you have to take care of Balder?"

"I groomed him and shoveled his stall before breakfast," said Vanessa. "So it's no trouble."

Her smug voice was loud enough for Steven to hear what she said.

"That's a good attitude! Spoken like a true horse lover!" He smiled approvingly. "Always extend a helping hand, that's my motto."

I clenched my fists with irritation. Talk about buttering somebody up! I couldn't believe that Steven didn't see through her act. But he had such a big smile on his face you'd think he had won a great jumping event or something. I stomped into Hero's stall and started brushing him with angry, rapid strokes. I saw some stripes in a couple of places on his coat, kind of like sweat stripes. But I had brushed him very well yesterday after riding him, so he couldn't possibly be sweaty. It had to be

something else, I thought vaguely, my mind preoccupied with my irritation over Vanessa and how she'd managed to manipulate people and make them see her as a benevolent soul.

When I had finished brushing Hero and his coat was all nice and shiny, I took a deep breath and put my arms around his neck.

"Maybe I should make one last attempt at explaining to her that it wasn't my fault you were sold..." I said to my pony. He gave a low, contented snort as I stroked my hand across his nose, and I was filled with a warm feeling of love for him. Then I noticed another, unwelcome sting of pity for Vanessa.

"But I don't want to feel sorry for her," I said into Hero's ear. "She's trying to destroy everything for me at this camp, even though I haven't done anything to her."

Hero shook his head and snorted. Was he disagreeing with me?

"I know you love her and that she's good to you," I said, stroking his bangs away from his eyes, "but she's not nice to me, and I have a bad feeling that she's up to something. At least I'm going to be on my guard when we ride out today, that's for sure!"

But as it turned out I didn't need to wait until our ride for something bad to happen. After we had saddled up the horses and were ready to go, I noticed that Hero was walking a little funny. Was he limping? I felt Vanessa's eyes on me as I slid down from the saddle to check. Hero was standing with one of his front hooves partially raised, so that only the toe part of his shoe touched the ground. I checked his hoof and saw a fairly big, sharp stone wedged in between the sole and the hoof. How did that get there? We had barely started walking and I had cleaned his hooves thoroughly yesterday, hadn't I? For a moment I wasn't sure. Was it possible that I had skipped one of his front hooves? No, that's not possible – or was it...?

"What's the matter?" asked Steven and came over to me.

"Hero has a big, sharp stone in his hoof," I said, feeling my face getting warm and flushed. "I don't understand how it got there."

"Did you remember to clean his hooves last night?" Steven looked at me.

"Yes!" I said. "Or... I'm sure I checked them... at least I think I did..."

"Poor Hero, I hope he'll be all right!" I heard Vanessa say. "You should do what I do, Shannon. I always check the hooves before I ride, even if I know that I cleaned them out the night before."

"That's a good routine," nodded Steven. "Better to check once too often than once too few!"

He lifted Hero's leg. "It looks like this rock has been here for a while. You couldn't possibly have cleaned his hooves properly last night!"

His voice was neither warm nor friendly now, and I didn't dare to look at him. My heart started beating faster, and it didn't feel good. This was horrible! What if Hero had gone lame? And it would be my fault! But I'm always so careful about cleaning his hooves! How could I have forgotten this time? I started feeling sick to my stomach, and wasn't even able to feel annoyed that Vanessa once again tried to score points with Steven by tooting her own horn. While Steven removed the rock, I glanced over at her. Her face showed a strange mixture of malice and anger.

"There!" Steven said, satisfied. "The rock is gone! Why don't you lead him around a little, Shannon, so I can see if he's limping."

My hands were shaking as I grabbed the reins and started walking, nervously awaiting Steven's judgment.

When his voice finally called out, "He looks fine," I was so relieved that I almost started laughing. But the laughter stifled in my throat, as Steven continued, "Let this be a lesson to you, Shannon! You must never shirk your duty when it comes to checking your horse's hooves! Forgetting to brush your horse one day won't cause a disaster, but a sharp rock that's wedged in the way this one was

could actually damage the hoof. So don't let me see this happen again, either with you or the rest of you. Learn from Vanessa! It's better to be safe than sorry!"

Needless to say, the group ride wasn't much fun for me after this incident. It felt as if everyone was looking at me and whispering behind my back. At least Vanessa and Chelsea were doing that. They were riding side by side, chatting, and every so often they turned around and gave me a look that made me cringe. At some point Vanessa slowed down and fell behind in the line, clearly in order to wait for me. I tried to avoid looking at her as I passed her, but I couldn't avoid hearing what she said.

"I knew you didn't deserve Hero," she said. "You can't even manage something as simple as checking his hooves! If he were mine, this never would have happened, I can guarantee that! But a spoiled

Daddy's girl like you, who gets everything she wants, probably doesn't understand that there are responsibilities that come with owning a horse!"

Her words hit me like an arrow in the chest. She called me a spoiled Daddy's girl? Me? I didn't even have a daddy, except in old pictures. I don't know why those particular words hurt me so much, because I never even knew my father. And you can't miss someone you've never met, can you? But right then I wished, suddenly and vehemently, that he had never gone on that ill-fated drive that had killed him. How would my life have been if the accident had never happened? We would probably have been living in a different place, and I may not have gotten a pony...

I hardly ever think about my dad, but now a string of strange thoughts, "what ifs," kept churning in my head, and I felt a strange longing that I could not remember ever having felt before.

"It's probably just because I'm lonely and not having a very good time right now," I told myself. Maybe I should call my mom after all? This is not much fun!

I had fallen behind the riding group and let them get way ahead of me without even noticing it. And here I was, waiting for Haley to come back. I still didn't know what to say to her. If I told her how much it bothered me to have Vanessa hate me so much, she would probably think I was stupid and childish and wimpy. But it sounded like she was planning to ride with me, and that was something. I felt my mood lighten a little. This was exactly what I had been hoping for when I signed up for the camp. And just this morning, before breakfast, I had talked to Hannah and bragged about how much fun it was here. What would she say if I came crawling back home just because a couple of girls had been mean to me? Hannah would never ever have let anybody ruin a camp like this for her. She had about a thousand times more self-confidence than I have. Maybe I should keep trying to think, "what would Hannah do?" every time Vanessa came around with one of her malicious, little jabs. Yes, that was a good plan! I would try to pretend as if I was Hannah, and downright borrow some of her self-assurance... Of course, the problem was that I wasn't anything like Hannah at all, so I was probably bound to fail...

This is how I kept thinking back and forth the whole time until Haley came back. She was gone for quite a while and I started getting worried that she might have forgotten about me (there was that low self-esteem again!), but finally I heard the sound of a horse approaching, and soon after Haley showed up.

"Sorry I took so long," she said. "The others had gotten much further than I thought. I gave Steven the impression that

you were right behind the group, and told him that you and I had agreed to take a ride by ourselves. I hope that's okay with you?"

Okay?? It was more than okay! Suddenly all my gloominess went away. There was plenty of time to worry about my problems later. Right now I was going to live in the moment and enjoy this opportunity to ride with my idol. I couldn't believe that she had actually initiated this! It was fantastic!

"That's better!" said Haley, when she saw the smile on my face. "You looked so sad and miserable a moment ago, I got worried. Do you want to talk about it...?"

"It's nothing, really," I said, evasive. "I've never been to a camp by myself before, and I guess I felt a little lonely and homesick."

I felt a little guilty about lying to Haley, but I didn't feel like talking about Vanessa. At least not now, when everything was so nice. It would just ruin my mood again, and I definitely didn't want that.

"I know how you feel," said Haley as we steered the horses down a trail to the left from where the riding group had gone. "First camp on your own can be tough. I know all about that!"

"You do?" I could tell how surprised I sounded. I wouldn't have thought that Haley had ever had problems with any-

thing at all, as confident and comfortable as she always seemed to be.

"You bet!" Haley laughed. "I always used to have my big brother come with me to camps and events and stuff, every time, until I became a teenager. If it hadn't been for him, I probably wouldn't have become a competitive rider at all, because my parents never had the time to get involved with my interest in riding. They're both doctors with very busy jobs, so I don't blame them, at least not now that I'm older and almost a grown-up myself. And I did have my brother as a helper and role model. He was a very competent show jumper. But when I turned thirteen he left for college. The first event where I had to manage on my own was horrible. I was sharing a room with another girl whom I disliked so much I just wanted to go home. She kept criticizing me the whole time."

Haley bent forward and patted Lotus on the neck. "Fortunately I was stubborn enough to stay. If I had chickened out and gone home, as I really wanted to, I might never have dared to go to any more events, and that would have been it for my riding career. So I'm glad I stuck it out. I still remember the great feeling I had when the last day was over, though."

"Did you win?" I asked excitedly.

Haley shook her head. "No, that nasty girl I shared a room with beat me in the

tiebreaker round. I was the fastest, but had a subtle knockdown on one of the hurdles. She rode faultless. It was a little hard to take at the time, but she was two years older than I was, and I'd proven that I was good enough, regardless."

Haley looked at me. "When I went home from that event I had gained new confidence in myself and my skills. And do you know what? Last year I competed against that same girl again. By then we were both a little more grown up, and she told me that she had been so mean because she knew I was going to be better than she was. Now I can just laugh at the whole thing, but I'm telling you, it was rough while I was in the middle of it. Sometimes you just have to grin and bear it. Running away from problems doesn't do any good."

Was Haley telepathic? I had a feeling she hadn't told me this story by coincidence. Was it possible that she had seen some of the things that had taken place between Vanessa and me? I wanted to ask her, but decided not to. She had given me a lot to think about, though. And I already knew she was right. If I went home now I would feel like a loser, and Vanessa would have achieved what she wanted. So I had to stay, whether I liked it or not.

And right now life didn't seem all that bad anyway. This ride with Haley was something I would remember for a long time. After the initial disappointment of the first couple of days when she had seemed distant, she had come through and been every bit as nice as I had thought she would be. And she wasn't some super-human as I had thought. She had felt timid and afraid once, too. It was good to know that. I always tend to think that others are so much surer of themselves and that I'm the only one who's not. But that's not how it is, of course, Haley had just showed me that.

Haley smiled and bent forward to pat Lotus on the neck. Lotus lifted her head and flapped her ears. There was something expectant in her eyes, I thought.

"She looks like she's looking forward to something," I said.

"Oh, she probably wants to do another gallop," laughed Haley. "We practice jumping so much, and she loves to jump, but to her there's nothing better than a real nice run. Then she's as happy as a horse can be! What do you say, should we let our horses stretch their legs a little? This trail is designed for a good gallop."

I glanced down at Hero. He seemed a little out of it, as if he wasn't quite up to snuff. I felt a sudden pang of worry again.

"I'm not sure," I said, a little hesitant. "Normally Hero can hardly wait for a chance to gallop. But today it's almost as if his engine's running on empty. Do you think he might be sick or something?"

Haley looked searchingly at Hero. "He doesn't look particularly sick," she said. "His eyes are clear and alert, he's not sweating, and he doesn't seem to be bothered by anything. And from what I could tell while we were walking, he doesn't seem to have a problem with his legs. I don't think you need to worry. It could just be that he's having some problems being in an unfamiliar stable and new surroundings. Some horses are strange that way. A friend of mine actually had to switch horses because of it. His horse got so uneasy and simply could not relax whenever they went to events and stuff. And of course that had an effect on their

results too, because a tired, uneasy horse can't perform its best."

"You're probably right," I said, relieved. "I thought he settled in very nicely at the stable here, because in a way he's used to being moved. I only got him a couple of months ago. But maybe it works the other way. Maybe he got unsettled by being moved again and had to get used to yet another new stable."

"Could very well be," nodded Haley. "It's too bad horses can't talk, then we could ask them if they need an extra pillow or something to help with their beauty sleep."

I pictured Hero lazily lounging on a pile of pillows, and started laughing.

"C'mon," Haley said, smiling. "I don't think a little run will hurt him. If he doesn't feel like it you'll know, and then of course we'll stop."

She seated herself deeper in the saddle and spurred Lotus into a gallop. The well-trained horse wasn't slow to respond. He lunged forward as if he had a rocket on his heels.

"C'mon, Hero," I urged. "You don't want Lotus to run away from you, do you?"

Hero seemed unwilling and hesitant at first, but after he had galloped for a little while he seemed to get back to his normal, energetic self. He stepped out as briskly as ever, and we actually started gaining on Lotus and Haley. I was so relieved by the change in him that I laughed out loud. The sense of the strong, muscular horse that carried me forward faster and faster was incredibly wonderful. Feeling the wind against my cheeks, seeing the trail disappear under the thundering hooves and knowing that this was my very own pony who ran so lightly and effortlessly with me on his back, made pure joy bubble up inside me. At that moment all my grief and worries were forgotten by sheer delight at the fact that I – the shy and wimpy Shannon – was racing with none other than Haley Larson! Too bad nobody was around to take a picture of us. But that didn't really matter. Some experiences you remember forever, and I knew that this magical moment was one I would never forget.

Chapter 6

False Accusations

"Are you telling me that you've managed to lose Hero's bridle?" Steven looked at me with disbelief.

I shook my head, feeling both irritated and resigned. "That's not what I'm saying," I said. "I'm only trying to tell you that the bridle is gone! I put it on the shelf over there because I was going to wash it after dinner, and now it's not there!"

"Well, a bridle doesn't just disappear into thin air." Steven scratched his head. "You'll just have to keep looking until you find it! I don't have time for this right now. I have a stable full of horses who are waiting impatiently to get fed."

"Do you want me to help you feed them?" I offered, in an attempt to appease Steven. "I can look for the bridle later."

"No thanks, I'll be fine. You just go and find your bridle, and take better care of your things from now on, would you?" Steven turned on his heel and walked out of the saddle room. Feeling small and dispirited, I followed him.

What Steven had said hurt, and I felt that I was being treated very unfairly. I had put the bridle on the shelf, I was sure of it. My memory couldn't be that far off, could it?

"You probably dropped it in a corner and forgot it," said Vanessa in an acidic tone of voice. She was standing in the hallway with Chelsea and looked a lot like the smug cat who just swallowed the canary. "Just like you forgot to check Hero's hooves. You're not very good at taking care of your pony or his things, are you? If you had washed his bridle and put it where it belongs right away, like I did, then this wouldn't have happened."

The last part she said in a loud voice, probably to make sure Steven could hear it. My stomach tightened into a knot.

"I'll help you look," said Chelsea unexpectedly. "The bridle has to be here somewhere. I'll take another look around the saddle room, while you start searching the stable."

She turned her back on Vanessa and hurried down the hallway.

"Thank you, that's really nice of you," I yelled after her.

"Chelsea sure is a funny one," I thought bewildered. First she was being nice to me, then she ganged up with Vanessa and turned against me, and now she was nice to me again. Maybe she had finally started seeing through Vanessa. One could always hope.

I started searching the hallway very carefully. But of course there was no bridle there. And I had absolutely no hope that Chelsea would find it in the saddle room either, because I had looked everywhere in there. So were could it be?

As if on cue, I heard Steven's voice, "I found the bridle, Shannon! It's in here, with Hero."

I ran over to the stall. Steven had just brought in a bundle of hay for my horse, and Hero attacked the food with such vehemence, he showed no regard for Steven's feet. Steven had to take a quick jump back to save his toes. You'd think my pony had gone without food for days! It actually looked extremely funny, and I couldn't help laughing. But that was a mistake. Steven pursed his lips and didn't look happy at all. Apparently he didn't think it was the slightest bit funny. I guess I wouldn't have either if it were my toes that had almost been crushed!

Without saying a word, Steven pointed toward the floor of the stall. There was the bridle, partially covered under the straw. If

you didn't know any better, it would look as if I had dropped the bridle on the floor and forgotten it, and then Hero had kicked straw over it while it was lying there.

But I would never ever have tossed the bridle aside on the floor like that! I knew that with 100% certainty. Somebody had put it there, and it wasn't very hard to guess who. I grabbed the bridle. And now I was fuming inside. I was so furious that I totally forgot to thank Steven for finding it. Maybe that was just as well, because I would probably just have gotten another lecture about how disappointed he was that I had treated Hero's bridle that way.

With angry strides, I marched up to Vanessa and stuck the bridle under her face.

"You weren't by any chance the one who put this in Hero's stall, were you?" I asked, carefully keeping my voice low. I didn't want Steven to hear what I was saying. He would probably lose it completely if he heard me accuse the wonderful Vanessa of something like this.

"Me? Don't be silly!" But her malicious smirk told me the truth.

"You might as well admit it," I hissed irately. "I know it was you! I can see it in your face!"

"Prove it!" Vanessa tossed her head with a scornful expression.

"I can't prove it, but don't you ever try something like this again!"

I turned on my heel and left her without waiting for an answer.

It wasn't easy to fall asleep that night. I was confused and anxious and didn't know what to do. The bed was soft and comfy, but I couldn't relax. I had a prickly feeling all over my body, as if it was covered in ants, and I had an awful feeling that something bad was going to happen. I tried to tell myself that I shouldn't think like that, but it was no use.

It had not been a particularly great evening, but that wasn't the reason why I felt so jittery right now, was it? It had started out so well, with Chelsea helping me wash the bridle and continuing to be friendly even though it clearly bothered Vanessa.

But afterwards Chelsea had gone to bed early. Apparently she hadn't slept very well the night before. She looked really tired too, but I was still wishing that she had stayed a little longer. While Chelsea and I talked, I hadn't noticed how Vanessa was buttering up Haley. But after Chelsea left, I discovered the two of them sitting close together, with Vanessa talking up a storm. Every now and then she glanced in my direction, and I wondered with horror what she might be saying to Haley. We had had such a good time together on the ride, and Haley had taken me seriously and given me some good advice. It had felt to me that she liked me, but now Vanessa would probably ruin that too. Soon, Haley would be looking at me with the same indifferent gaze that Steven had offered me all night. I had been contemplating whether I should talk to Steven and try to make him see that I wasn't the

one who had tossed the bridle aside in the stall. But when I saw how unsympathetic he seemed, I gave up the idea. He wouldn't believe me anyway, even if I didn't tell him that I suspected Vanessa was behind it. I chatted with a couple of the other campers for a while, but they were discussing films and books I had never even heard of, so I just felt stupid and in the way. In the end I went out to the stable, saddled up Hero and took a short, peaceful ride. Hero seemed perky and rested and looked like he enjoyed our little extra outing. I tried to enjoy it as well, but just couldn't quite relax and have a good time, as I usually do when we go riding. Too many distressing thoughts were going through my mind.

Afterwards I brushed Hero and cuddled with him at length, and then I went up to my room and called Hannah. Last time I talked to her I had let on that everything was fun, and I started doing the same thing this time. I told her about my wonderful ride with Haley, and Hannah said I'd better watch out, or else the ugly, green color of her growing jealousy would start oozing out of my cell phone!

I laughed and we talked some more about Haley, but the whole time I had a hard knot in my stomach because of all the other things that were going on. Suddenly I couldn't stand to pretend anymore. All the bad stuff that had happened started pouring out of me, and I told Hannah how much Vanessa hated me.

"But that's completely unfair!" Hannah burst out when I finally stopped. "How is it your fault that Hero was sold?"

"I know, and that's exactly what I've been trying to say to her too! But she won't listen. She's determined to ruin the camp for me. I'm sure she's talking about me behind my back. And now she's started doing other things too. I'm afraid that this incident with the bridle is just the beginning!"

That's when Hannah said something that I now couldn't get out of my head as I was lying in bed, tossing and turning.

"Have you considered the idea that the bridle incident wasn't the beginning? What if she planted the rock in Hero's shoe?"

"Are you crazy?" I shook my head, even though I knew Hannah couldn't see it. "She's after me, but she would never do anything to hurt Hero."

"Are you sure about that?" said Hannah. "Just think about it – you're almost ridiculously careful when it comes to taking care of your pony. I don't believe for a second that you forgot to check his hooves. If so, it must have been a case of temporary insanity, or whatever it's called."

I sat there nodding to myself without interrupting Hannah. This was exactly what I had been thinking too, but the idea that somebody had sabotaged my pony on purpose hadn't occurred to me. Surely that couldn't be true!

But after I had gone to bed, the thought wouldn't go away. If I had cleaned his hooves properly, and deep down I was quite sure I had, then how did the rock get in there? Steven had said it definitely didn't come from the stable yard, and that was the only place Hero had been. There were no rocks in his stall, and the hallway was always cleaned before any of the horses came out of their stalls...

But would Vanessa really do something like that? One moment I was sure she absolutely would not. The next moment I thought about how much she hated me, so maybe... But if she really had done it, then what might she do next?

I didn't even want to think about it. And the worst thing was, nobody would ever believe me or help me. Actually, maybe Chelsea would, but I didn't trust her any more, after seeing how incredibly unpredictable she was. Talk about split personality! I gave a heavy-hearted sigh as I got up and went into the bathroom to get a drink of water. Should I call Hannah and talk to her some more? But when I realized that it was almost twelve a clock already, I dropped the idea. Hannah was probably asleep by now, and it would take more than the skimpy sound from a cell

phone to wake her up. On school mornings, her mom usually has to drag her out of bed, and that's after Hannah's slept through the obnoxious ringing from two alarm clocks. There was no way she would wake up if I called her cell phone.

I sighed, rolled over and tucked the covers around me. Two seconds later I was too hot and threw the covers off, but then it got too cold again, so I pulled them back on once more. I kept doing this for what seemed like an eternity, my mind in a complete turmoil. Then I must have fallen asleep, because suddenly I was standing in the stable, desperately holding onto Hero while I yelled in despair, "No! You can't take him away from me! He's mine!" Standing in a circle around me were Steven, Mom, Grandma and Vanessa. All of them had a stern, serious look on their faces. Steven reached his arm out and tried to pull me away from Hero, while Mom said in a sad voice, "We realize now that you can't take care of your pony – you don't groom him or anything. Just see for yourself!"

I looked at Hero. He was shaggy, dirty and had long, uneven hooves with big cracks in them. How did he get like this?

"It's not my fault!" I cried.

"Let go of him!" commanded Steven. "We're giving Hero to somebody who deserves him."

Before I knew what had happened, he

had a firm grasp around me, while Vanessa triumphantly led Hero out of the stable. And suddenly the pony was all pretty and properly groomed again.

"See there," said Steven. "Vanessa's already taken care of him! She is a responsible horse owner and not a slacker like you!"

"But everything is her fault!" I screamed.

Nobody cared about what I said, no matter how much I screamed and tried to pull free, and all I could do was stand there and watch as Hero left the stable and my life. I heard the sound of horse's hooves on the ground outside...

... and woke up, totally soaked in sweat. For one horrible moment I wondered if it was true. Had they given Hero to Vanessa? But then I realized that it was only a dream, a horrible dream. Hero was still mine, and he was standing safely in his stall.

But part of the dream continued. The muted sound of horse's hooves was still there, very faint, but audible. It took me a few seconds to realize that the sound wasn't just in my head. It was real, and came from outside through the open window. Horse's hooves, at this time, in the middle of the night? I had no idea what time it was, but it was still pretty dark out.

Still half-dazed from that awful dream, I jumped out of bed and walked quietly to the window. I pulled the curtain aside, then gasped in surprise. On the other side of the stable, over by the arena, I could see the outline of a horse with a rider on his back. I strained my eyes to see better. Was there another rider too, a little further away? I wasn't sure. But who in the world would be outside, riding at this time of night when normal people are asleep? It had to be someone who didn't want to be seen. And suddenly it dawned on me. The Night Riders! I had managed to suppress the scary story Haley had told us, but now it came back to me in full force. The Night Riders! What if they had come to take one of us away? Vanessa, Chelsea and I were the youngest people at the ranch right now. We weren't small children, but still... I felt my body turn icy cold. It was spooky to stand here in the dark room and look out at the silent riders approaching. Or was it just one rider? It didn't matter. Maybe the Night Riders only send out one to fetch the prey. Nobody knew anything about who – what – they were. And my window was open! I was scared stiff as I pictured a nondescript, dark figure stretching toward the window, grabbing hold of me, and pulling me away... to what exactly? To be a slave for the Night Riders? Or something even worse...? With a gasp I slammed the window shut and turned the lock. Then I checked to see if my door was locked before I jumped into bed and

must have fallen asleep eventually, because all of a sudden it was morning and bright sunlight – and stifling hot in the room! I felt as stupid as stupid gets when I tottered out of bed and walked over to open the window again. Talk about being hysterical! This was the second time I'd carried on like an idiot because of that silly story about The Night Riders. Even Haley had said, when she told the story, that she didn't believe in it.

But I had seen a rider, or possibly two... hadn't I? In the night I had been sure, but now all of a sudden I wasn't. It could have been some bushes or trees. After all, everything looks different in semi-darkness... And the sounds that I had heard, had they really been there, or did I only imagine them because of the dream?

While I was standing in the shower I decided that I must have imagined the whole thing. At least I'm not going to tell anybody about this, that's for sure, I thought as I closed the door to my room and went down for breakfast. Would Chelsea be nice today again? I wondered. I hoped so. But either way, I was looking forward to our jumping lesson with Haley. At least I wasn't going to let anybody ruin that part for me...

pulled the covers over my head. I was lying there, trembling, listening intently for any sounds. But now that I had closed the window it was impossible to hear anything but my own heartbeats, which thumped all the way up in my ears. I have no idea how long I was lying there like that, afraid that somebody was coming to get me. But as hard as it is to believe, I

Chapter 7

Trouble

"Shannon! Come here, please!"

Steven's voice practically banged in my ears. He sounded furious.

I turned around, astonished. Steven looked no less angry than he sounded. I couldn't fathom why. I hadn't overslept or done anything I shouldn't have, as far as I knew.

"What is it? Is something wrong?"

"How can you even ask that?" Steven put his hands on his hips and gave me a look that made it clear I was way down on his list of favorite people. "I was just over at the stable, and what do you think I found there?"

"Ho... horses?" I stammered, frightened. Steven's face looked like a thundercloud, and I realized that he must have thought I was trying to be funny. But that was as far from the truth as could be. Something was very, very wrong, and I had no idea what.

"Is it... is something wrong with Hero?" I asked with increasing worry.

"Not if you're in the habit of leaving your pony all dirty and unkempt, with sweat marks all over him! If you have to go for late night rides, you should, for one thing, ride him sensibly, and secondly, take the time to groom him afterwards!"

"I don't understand what you're talking about," I tried to say. "Hero was fine when I left him last night, and..."

"Don't give me a bunch of lame excuses," hissed Steven. "First you neglect to check the your pony's hooves, and then you leave your bridle lying around everywhere, and now this! I am speechless! If you want to be a horse owner, you need to show more responsibility than this. I'm truly disappointed in you, Shannon! Disappointed and angry!"

I felt like I was in the middle of a bad dream again. This could not be happening! But it was, and right in front of everybody. Steven hadn't exactly lowered his voice as he spoke to me, and several of the

campers had come closer to find out what was going on. Closest of them all was, of course, Vanessa. She looked almost as mad as Steven, but when I met her eyes, I was suddenly convinced that whatever it was that had happened, Vanessa was behind it.

But right then I didn't have time to worry about that. First I had to find out what had happened to Hero. I rushed out of the house and over to the stable. A big lump in my throat made it hard to swallow, and tears were burning in my eyes. This was horrible! I knew very well that I had brushed Hero thoroughly after my ride, but I had been alone in the stable, so how could I prove it?

When I saw Hero, however, the despair I had felt was instantly replaced by fury. My poor pony stood there with his head hanging low, looking totally exhausted. This had gone too far! How could Vanessa do something like this to a pony she claimed to love?

Hero hadn't been sweaty at all after our ride last night, but now his coat was completely stained, as if he had been ridden very hard or had been terrified. The look of his legs indicated the former, because they were covered in mud and... pine needles? Had Vanessa been riding my pony in the woods – in the dark? Suddenly I remembered the rider I thought I had seen and heard in the night. So it hadn't just

been my imagination! Vanessa had been out with Hero!

I thought about how tired he had seemed yesterday. Had the same thing happened the night before too? Was Vanessa taking him out for rides at night? Was that how he had gotten that rock in his hoof? The more I thought about it, the angrier I got.

"She's gonna get it, if it's the last thing I do!" I fumed, while hurrying into the saddle room to get my grooming tools.

When I got back to the stall, Steven was there, with Vanessa. I gave Vanessa a murderous look as I pushed past her into the stall, without uttering a word. I had plenty to say to her later, but not now while Steven was there.

"Let's just hope your carelessness doesn't result in Hero getting a cold or worse," said Steven in a dismal voice. "I can't understand how you could..."

"But I didn't!" I interrupted angrily. "Can't you hear what I'm saying? Hero was fine when I left him! Somebody else took him out and rode him last night!"

"It would have been better if you'd admitted the truth instead of making up some story," said Steven, resigned.

I didn't answer, but started brushing Hero with long, slow strokes. He lowered his head and closed his eyes, looking as if he was about to fall asleep with pure pleasure. Or was it because he was so

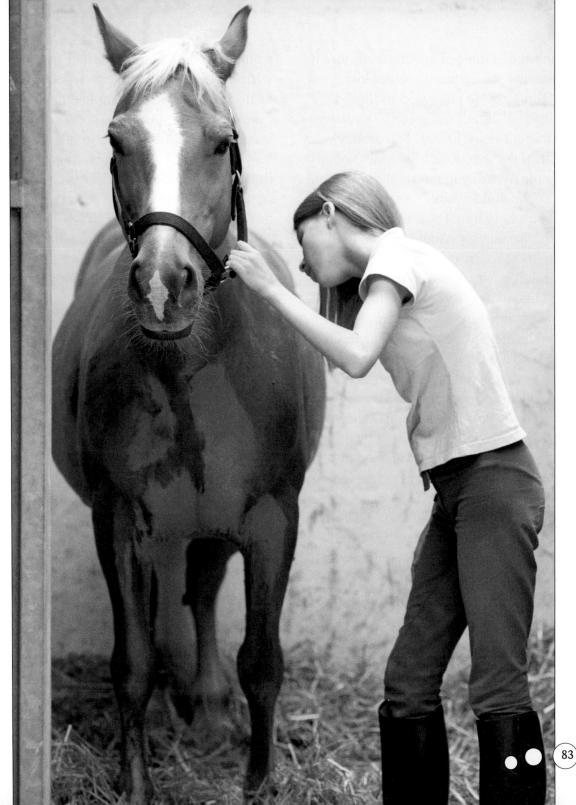

exhausted? I noticed another lump in my throat and put my arms around him.

"I'm going to put a stop to this," I whispered. "She's not going to bother you anymore, I'll see to that! You are my pony, and I'm going to look after you. Nobody is going to take you out riding in the middle of the night again!"

The whole time I was taking care of Hero, Steven was standing in the hallway with his arms crossed, as if he thought I might drop the brush and run away if he left to go and do something else. I decided to pretend that I didn't see him.

Fortunately Vanessa had gone to take care of Balder, but she wasn't going to get away with this! I'd had enough, more than enough! And what if Hero got sick from all this? I hadn't even thought about that until Steven said it. If he did, I would never forgive Vanessa! I was mad at Steven too. He said he was disappointed in me, but I was every bit as disappointed in him! All right, so he didn't know me, but why was he so quick to think the worst about me? After all, he didn't know Vanessa either, but even so he seemed to think she was a saint, just because she made sure to say and do the right things whenever he was nearby. It was totally unfair!

I had just packed away my grooming tools when Haley came into the stable. My heart just about sank to my stomach. What would she think about me when she heard what happened – or rather – when she heard what Steven thought had happened? I didn't have to wait long, because Steven instantly started unloading to her about how he'd arrived at the stable this morning to find Hero in a terrible state.

"I have a good mind to send her home this instant," he finally said.

I dropped my shoulders and didn't dare to look at Haley. Now she'd probably disapprove of me as well, if she hadn't already after whatever Vanessa had said to her about me last night. And Steven wanted to send me home! I might as well go inside and call my mom. I certainly didn't want to stay here anymore!

But Haley surprised me. "I'm not sure you should be so quick to draw conclusions," she said to Steven. "If Shannon says that she did take proper care of Hero, and that somebody else must have ridden her pony, then why don't you believe her?"

"Because she has proven time and again that she's unreliable," said Steven short. "And why would anybody else be riding her pony in the middle of the night?"

"That I don't know," said Haley calmly. "But I do know Shannon well enough after these few days to know she wouldn't have ridden her pony really hard and then left him all sweaty and muddy afterwards.

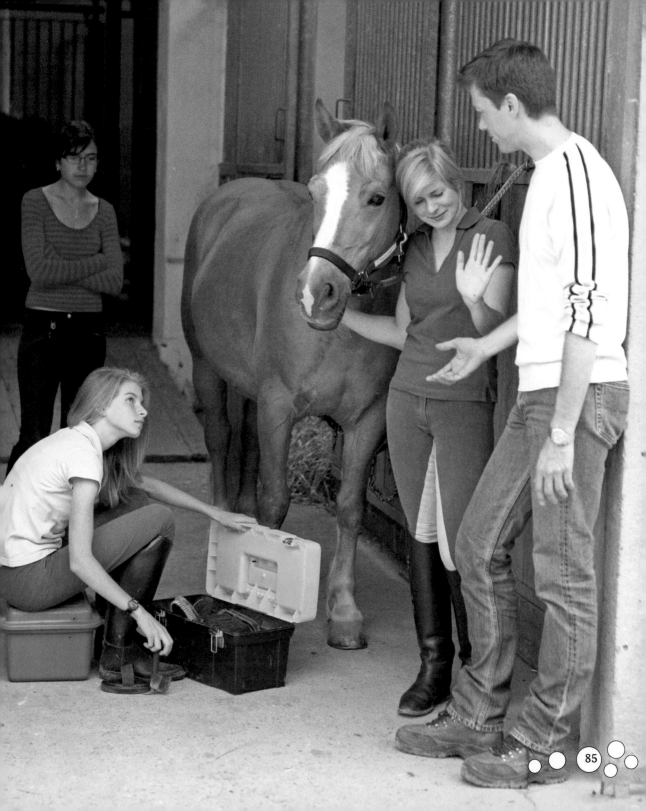

I think you should listen to her and try to find out what really happened, instead of threatening to send her home!"

I felt like throwing my arms around Haley's neck and giving her a crushing hug in gratitude. Finally, somebody who believed in me!

There was a long silence. Steven's face had turned red and he looked very uncomfortable. I glared at him, but he wouldn't look at me. It was very clear that he felt bad.

"I'm sorry if I've been unfair," he finally said, directed at my shoes.

I didn't answer. Surely he didn't think that he could just mumble some lame excuse and then everything would be all right? *If* he had been unfair, he had said. It didn't really sound as if he meant to say sorry at all. He was probably doing it just because Haley had demanded it.

Vanessa had stood by silently and listened to everything, and I had almost forgotten that she was there. But out of the corner of my eye I saw her move, and turned my head. Vanessa was on her way into Balder's stall. Did she think she could hide in there? Did she really think that I didn't know she was the one who had done this?

The relief I had felt a moment ago when Haley supported me was replaced by a seething fury. I pushed my way past Steven without paying any attention to him.

"How could you do that to Hero?" I asked with stifled anger. "It can be dangerous to ride in the dark! Don't you know that? What if he'd been injured? What were you thinking?"

"What?" Vanessa's mouth fell open as she looked at me.

"Don't even try to act innocent," I said. "I know perfectly well it was you!"

"What are you talking about? Are you crazy?" Vanessa looked at me with narrow eyes. "Are you trying to blame this on me?"

"Of course it was you!" I hissed. I was so angry I was shaking. "You are so jealous, it's pathetic! You can't stand the idea that Hero is my pony and not yours! But this is going too far! You claim to love Hero so much, but it sure doesn't seem like it! I have a good mind to..."

"Hey! Stop that!" Steven's voice interrupted my tirade. "You can't just throw accusations around like that..."

"And that's supposed to come from you?" I turned toward Steven with a look that made his face red again. "You don't hesitate for a second to accuse me of all kinds of things."

"I've already apologized for that," said Steven. He sounded more irritated than sorry. "But you have no reason to think that Vanessa has anything to do with this."

Vanessa glanced at me with an expression that seemed like sheer malice to me.

That was the drop that made the cup run over. I didn't wait to hear another word. I turned on my heel and ran out of the stable. This was hopeless! Nothing I said mattered at all! Steven was so blinded by Vanessa that he probably wouldn't have believed anything bad about her even if I could prove it, I thought, despairing.

I heard Haley call out to me, but I didn't stop to find out what she wanted.

Later, as I lay on my bed, I felt guilty about that. Haley was the only one who had supported me. What if she got mad at me for having left without answering her? I would try to find her later and tell her I was sorry. Haley might be able to help me. If I could convince her that it was Vanessa who had taken Hero out in the night, maybe we could set a trap...

I lay on my back with my hands under my head. I was still fuming inside. Why couldn't Steven see through Vanessa's act and realize what she was really like?

I have no idea how long I was lying there pondering, but I must have dozed off eventually, because when someone knocked at the door I was in the middle of a dream where Vanessa and I were standing on opposite sides of Hero, tugging at his bridle and yelling, "he's mine!"

I sat up, feeling confused. There was another knock, and I called, "come in!"

I had kind of expected to see Haley, but it was Chelsea who came into the room.

"Hi," she said quietly. "How's it going?" I shrugged my shoulders without saying anything.

"Steven sent me to ask if you feel like coming to the riding lesson after lunch."

I shrugged my shoulders again. There was an awkward moment of silence.

"Did he tell you what happened?" I finally asked.

Chelsea squirmed. She seemed ill at ease. "He said something about some mistakes..."

"Mistakes? That's a good one! Steven threatened to send me home!" I jumped out of bed so fast that Chelsea took a step backward. "Haley stopped him, but I could tell that he didn't really believe I was innocent. I just don't know how I can get him to see the truth about that witch!"

"What truth? What witch?"

Chelsea looked at me guardedly, as if I was a mad dog who could jump at her at any moment.

I dropped down on the bed again.

"Sorry, I didn't mean to yell at you. It's not your fault. I'm talking about Vanessa! She rode Hero last night and left him all sweaty and dirty, just so I would be blamed for it."

"Why are you so sure that it was her who did it?"

"Who else could it be? And I'm going to make her admit it! You just wait until I get her to myself!"

Chelsea didn't say anything. She looked down at the floor and it almost seemed like she wanted it to swallow her up. Didn't she believe me?

Well, it didn't really matter, I thought, trying to ignore a pang of disappointment. The important thing now was to catch Vanessa. The thought of how miserable Hero had looked this morning, covered in sweat and mud, made me determined to force the truth out of her. Exactly how to achieve it was not at all clear to me, however. But one thing was certain – she wasn't going to get away with this!

Chapter 8

Haley Saves the Day Again

It proved to be easier said than done to get Vanessa to myself. She wasn't in the stable when I came back to check on Hero. My pony was standing there all alone. Steven had taken all the other horses for a short ride, Haley told me. She came in with Lotus, putting him back in his stall.

"Steven isn't the kind of person who finds it easy to apologize, but I think he really is sorry that he was so hard on you," said Haley, when she came back out from the saddle room after having put her saddle and bridle away.

And so he should! I thought, though I didn't really believe what she said. I could tell that Steven still had doubts about my innocence.

Suddenly I had tears in my eyes. Everything that had happened over the last few days was too much for me, and when Haley put a hand on my shoulder and gave me a sympathetic smile, I couldn't hold back any longer. I threw my arms around Hero's neck and started sobbing.

"This has been the worst week of my entire life," I gasped into his mane. "Vanessa has been so mean to me, and Steven too, even though I haven't done anything wrong. I should never have come here! I want to go home!"

Hero stood still and accepted my flood of tears with patience. His mane was completely wet when I finally lifted my head, sniffled and started wiping my eyes. I jumped when I saw that Haley was still there. I guess I thought she would have gone by now. But she was standing quietly in the hallway looking at me. I felt my head get even warmer than it already was from all the crying. What must she think of me, standing here bawling like a crybaby?

"Feel better now?" she said softly.

I nodded, then fished out a tissue and blew my nose.

"C'mon," Haley said. "Let's give Hero some rest, and then you can help me

brush Lotus. She's been rolling around onthe ground and she's totally covered in dirt.

Haley went into Lotus's stall without waiting for an answer. I followed her hesitantly, blowing my nose again. In movies the heroine always gets delicately shiny eyes and sheds a few pretty tears. Afterwards she's just as beautiful as before. I was glad there wasn't a mirror around, because I knew that my eyes were as red as an albino rabbit's, and my face would be shiny and blotchy from all the crying.

But luckily Haley didn't comment on my crying or on the way I looked. She just handed me a brush, and then we started cleaning the dirt off of Lotus. While I brushed I felt completely empty-headed, and relieved in a way.

We worked for quite a while without saying anything, but finally Haley broke the silence.

"I hope you didn't mean what you said about wanting to go home," she said. "You know what I think about running away from problems. It doesn't solve anything. I think we should try to figure this all out instead."

She looked at me. "Those were some pretty serious accusations you hurled at Vanessa. What makes you so sure that she's the culprit behind the things that have happened to Hero?

"Because she hates me and is extremely jealous, even though it's not my fault that she didn't get to buy Hero!"

Then I blurted out everything that had happened since I'd arrived. Haley listened without interrupting once. When I was all done, she said: "Hmm! I understand now." She was silent for a moment. "I can see that Vanessa's made your life miserable here. But I do have a problem imagining her doing something that could actually hurt Hero."

"But it has to be Vanessa!" I objected, a little hurt that Haley was doubtful about what I had told her.

Haley didn't say anything for a while. "Maybe you're right," she finally said reluctantly. "Jealousy and envy can make people do things you'd never think they were capable of. But have you talked to Vanessa properly about this? Without screaming accusations at her, I mean."

I shook my head. "But I intend to," I continued, and told Haley that I was planning to get Vanessa to myself and force her to admit it.

"I guess it couldn't hurt to try," said Haley. "But don't be too disappointed if she refuses to admit anything at all. If she's the one who's behind all this, she must know that she's done something really stupid and dangerous, and she may not want to admit that, to herself or to anybody else."

There was that word "if" again! As if there was any doubt about it! But Haley, and all the others for that matter, could just keep doubting as much as they wanted. When Vanessa had confessed, they would be embarrassed that they hadn't trusted me more!

All I had to do now was wait until Vanessa came back from the group ride, and then I would wring the truth out of her. And afterwards, when Vanessa had been sent home, all the problems would go away along with her, and there would no longer be any reason for me to go home early. I was already looking forward to seeing her go home...

I waited impatiently for the riding group to come back, but when they finally arrived I still didn't get the chance to talk to Vanessa. The stable was a muddle of people scurrying about, unsaddling and taking care of their horses, and getting themselves ready for lunch. I kept away from Vanessa while we ate. It hurt to see Chelsea walk right past me and sit down next to her. If I had wondered whether Chelsea believed me or not when I told her what Vanessa had done, I certainly knew the answer now.

I ate quickly and went up to my room. I left the door open a crack and waited for Vanessa to come upstairs, hoping she would come soon and that she would be alone. If I didn't talk to her now, I would have to wait until after the riding lesson, which I didn't want to do. I was daydreaming about Vanessa, in her room packing to go home, while the rest of us had the jumping lesson with Haley. That would serve her right! She didn't deserve to get to train with Haley for another second, I thought, feeling vindictive.

There was Vanessa now! And she was alone. Nobody else was around. This was the chance I had waited for. I jumped into the hallway and stood in front of her, making her stop.

"What do you want?" she asked dismissively.

"To talk to you!"

"If you think I'm going to listen to any more of your wild accusations, you can think again. You are totally crazy, and I don't want to talk to you!"

Vanessa tried to elbow her way past me. I grabbed her arm.

"Oh, no! You're not going anywhere!" I pushed her into my room.

For a moment we just stood there, glaring at each other with hostility. Vanessa kept her mouth tightly shut, making it clear that she wasn't going to say a word.

I could hardly contain myself. I opened my mouth, intending to scream accusations at her, but then I thought about what Haley had said, and with great effort I managed to stop myself.

"I want you to admit what you've done and apologize for it," I said as calmly as I could. "If not for me, then for Hero's sake. If you love him at all, then you won't ever do something like this again! I want you to promise me that!"

"You really are crazy!" Vanessa looked angrily at me. "You can't seriously think that I've been riding Hero? I think you're just throwing around accusations left and right in order to hide the fact that you can't take care of your own pony! It's pathetic, that's what it is!"

"Don't you try that! I know it was you! Admit it, or else..."

"Or else what?" Vanessa shook her head contemptuously. "Nobody believes you anyway. You might as well give up all this nonsense. Why don't you take better care of Hero instead, and stop trying to blame it on others! All you do is whine and cry and play the innocent victim. You make me sick!"

Vanessa turned her back on me, flung the door open and strode out of the room. And I felt like the biggest fool in the world. How could I have been so naive to think that Vanessa would admit anything just because I told her to? And she was right, I couldn't prove anything. She hadn't given herself away with a single word. Instead she had pretended to think that I was behind the whole thing myself. Maybe she was afraid that I'd hidden somebody in the closet? A witness who could jump out as soon as she said anything revealing? Either way I was back at square one. What on earth was I going to do now?

I glanced at the clock and realized that I had to hurry if I was going to make it to the jumping lesson on time. But did I still want to go to it? Wouldn't it be better if I went home? I thought about what Haley had said about running away from your problems. But what if something happened to Hero again? What if Vanessa snuck into the stable and took him out again? And what if he ended up getting injured? I would never forgive myself if that happened. Reluctantly I picked up my cell phone. I could send Mom a text message and ask her to come and get me. Then I could still go to the riding lesson before I left. But just as I started keying the message, I got an idea, and it was a great idea. I could protect Hero from any further "kidnappings," and at the same time show Vanessa that I wasn't going to let her bully me away from here...

Chapter 9

Jumping Lesson With a Dream Horse

"Not bad, Shannon! You were almost completely in balance this time. Only a smidge too far forward in the landing, maybe. But all in all, you pass!"

Haley gave me a satisfied smile, and a tingle of joy spread throughout my body. This day, which had started out so horribly, had turned into the best experience I had had since Haley and I went for our ride together.

I had decided to not let anything ruin this riding lesson for me. It hadn't been easy, at least not in the beginning when I discovered that Hero was in absolutely no shape to jump over anything.

It was during our warm-up exercise that I noticed he wasn't up to it. Even the lowest hurdle, which he normally would have been able to jump blindfolded, he barely even made an attempt at.

"I guess we won't be able to do this lesson after all," I told Haley, my disappointment sitting like a heavy lump in my stomach. "Hero just doesn't feel up to it.

Somebody has seen to that!" I threw a stern look in Vanessa's direction. She turned away and pretended not to see me or my look.

"Yes, I can tell," said Haley. "Poor Hero! He must have been ridden really hard and long last night. I hope that if any of you know who did this, you'll come and talk to us, either to me or to Steven. It's not okay to steal a horse and treat it this way."

"But Hero wasn't stolen, was he?" commented Chelsea. "I mean, he was put back in the stable afterwards. And you make it sound like somebody abused him, but he's not hurt, so is it necessary to make such a big deal about it?"

I stared at Chelsea in shock and anger. What was the matter with her? Even if she didn't believe me with regard to Vanessa, she didn't have to downplay what had happened, did she?

"I most certainly think it's necessary to make a big deal about it," said Haley

sharply. "Nobody has a right to treat other people's horses like that. Or their own horse either, for that matter."

"But I don't see why you think it's any of us here at the riding camp who rode Hero," said Vanessa, putting on such an angel face that it made me sick. "Nobody who loves horses would dream of galloping around in the middle of the night on unknown ground, would they?"

A mumbling of agreement went through the group inside the arena.

Haley shrugged her shoulders. "You may be right, Vanessa," she said. "Either way we won't figure it out right now. But Hero can't jump, that much is certain. It's no good pushing him if he's not feeling up to it."

I tried to hide my disappointment as much as I could, but I think Haley understood how I felt, because she said, "Don't be sad, Shannon. Hero will be better soon. And you don't have to miss out on the jumping lesson. You can borrow another horse."

"I'll take Hero to his stall," offered Steven. He had been standing by the fence watching the warm-up. "I'll give him a few extra pellets, or maybe some warm oat grits. That's like an energy bomb."

I didn't respond because I was still mad at Steven, but instead handed him the reins and watched him lead Hero toward the stable.

I assumed that Steven would pick out another horse for me, but that's when Haley surprised me and turned the day into something totally special.

"I hope you don't mind a somewhat taller horse than what you're used to?" She held Lotus's reins out toward me. I gaped at her in astonishment. Did she mean...?

Haley nodded. "I'm sure Lotus will jump just fine for you. She's easy to handle in the arena. The only thing that will get her off balance is if you pull on her mouth. She has a very sensitive mouth. If you can just watch out for that, I'm sure you'll be fine."

My heart was beating like a drum as I got into the saddle. This was something I couldn't have come up with in my wildest imagination. But here I was, on top of Lotus, a famous horse that was considered just as great a talent as her owner. And Haley was going to let me ride this fantastic, and expensive, horse. I felt like I was floating. For a brief moment I also felt a little guilty about thinking that this was such a great thing. But only for a moment. It wasn't that I didn't think Hero was good enough. Because he was, more than good enough for me. But this was something totally unique. I think anybody who's been lucky enough to meet their long time idol knows what I mean.

I was filled with a mixture of awe and excitement as I spurred the large horse and steered her toward the first hurdle. She felt dangerously tall, and her back was wider than I was accustomed to with Hero.

Hence the first jump also almost ended badly. I got totally off balance and started sliding backward. Instinctively I wanted to tighten the reins, but remembered what Haley had said about Lotus having a sensitive mouth. So I pressed my legs against the horse and grabbed for the saddle instead. It felt like the jump across the hurdle lasted for an eternity, then Lotus landed so lightly and softly that you would never have thought that she had a completely inelegant and unbalanced rider on her back. I scrambled back into an upright position, my heart pounding against my chest. I was sure Haley would refuse to let me have any more tries. I didn't know if I even dared.

But Haley just laughed and told me to do it again!

"You were just too nervous and tense," she said. "I know it may be a little intimidating to ride Lotus because she's famous, but you know, she's still just a horse, and

she doesn't have any celebrity whims that you need to worry about. Just relax and try to follow her movements, and you'll be fine!"

I tried to do as Haley said. I did better the next time, and now, after five tries, my jump was almost perfect, according to Haley. I was on cloud nine. The look on Vanessa's face made the experience even better. You'd think she'd been forced to eat a truckload of extra bitter lemons or something. I knew she had meant to ruin the ride for me, but as a result I had been allowed to use this fantastic horse for the entire jumping lesson. It was like a dream come true.

After the lesson I hung around in the stable for a while, taking care of my own horse. Steven told me that Hero had eaten his oat grits with a greedy appetite, so he felt pretty sure that he wasn't getting sick. "Tomorrow Hero will be as good as new!" Steven smiled happily.

I felt almost numb with relief and returned his smile. Even though I still hadn't completely forgiven Steven, I couldn't stay angry either. That would have only affected me. I don't like being mad, and I was feeling as if I had been nothing but furious and sad for days. This afternoon, however, had been great, and things went all right at dinner too. I made sure to keep my distance from both Vanessa and Chelsea, and later, when I went into the stable again to say goodnight to Hero, I was in a good mood.

Hero was in his stall, standing there half asleep. He looked so cute, my heart swelled. I still had to pinch myself to be sure that this wonderful, loyal creature really belonged to me. As far as I was concerned, other people could just keep their marvelous purebred horses.

"You're the best in the world, you know that? No matter how fantastic Lotus might be, I wouldn't trade you for anything," I said as I patted my pony on the neck. "It was fun to sit on top of a star, but you and I suit each other much better!"

"Sit on top of a star! Gee! How sweet!" I turned around with a start. Vanessa and Chelsea were standing in the hallway. I hadn't been aware that they had followed me. Vanessa rolled her eyes, while Chelsea giggled. I felt a pang of hurt feelings. After Chelsea was so nice to me yesterday, I had hoped she'd continue to be nice, but today she was obviously taking Vanessa's side again. I had never come across anybody who behaved as unpredictably as Chelsea. It was as if she had two completely different sides and personalities...

I took a deep breath as I decided not to show how hurt I was.

"Why don't you ask Haley if you can ride Lotus too," I said with such a big and fake smile that I almost expected my face to crack. "Then you won't have to go around with that jealous, green color on your face. It's not very becoming!"

I just caught a glimpse of the stunned expression on Vanessa's face before I turned my back on her. She probably hadn't expected an answer like that. I started detangling Hero's mane with my fingers, as if nothing had happened.

But inside I was shaking, and wondering what Vanessa was going to do now. After all, they were two against one, and there was nobody else in the stable right now. I put my arms around Hero's neck and snuck a peek toward the stall door. To my surprise I heard Chelsea say, "C'mon, Vanessa, we don't feel like hanging around here. Let's go back to the house."

Shortly after, I heard the stable door

slam shut and I was alone with the horses. At first I was relieved, but then I started thinking. It wasn't like Vanessa to give up that easily and just walk away. And why did she and Chelsea come here in the first place? None of them had bothered to look in on their horses. Had Vanessa meant to visit Hero? And then she couldn't because I was here?

"I think she's up to something," I whispered to Hero. "And she doesn't want me to suspect anything. That's why she left."

Hero snorted and snatched another mouthful of hay. He didn't seem very interested in what I was saying. As long as he had enough food to eat, he couldn't care less about people's comings and goings!

"You may want to be a little bit worried," I said, scratching him on the forehead. "You're the one who will suffer, you know, if I can't manage to prevent it. But I have a plan..."

Hero flapped one ear as he continued to

chew, unperturbed. At least it didn't look like he had suffered any lasting damage from his nighttime outing. But that didn't mean that everything would end well the next time. And that's why I had to make sure that Vanessa didn't get another chance. I only needed a couple of things... I seemed to remember having seen some chains on a shelf in the saddle room. Sure enough! I smiled to myself while I sorted out the longest of them. If Vanessa tried anything tonight, she was in for a surprise! I was still smiling when I left the stable a while later. My plan was simple, but ingenious! At least that's what I thought then. If I had had the slightest idea of what the result would be, I may not have been quite so happy with myself.

Chapter 10

Horse Missing!

I didn't really count on sleeping very well that night, so I went to bed with the latest Horse Angel book, and started reading. The last thing I remember was thinking how nice it would've been if Angelica really existed, and Hero could call for her if he needed help...

... after which followed a muddle of confusing dreams of people hurrying through hallways and a buzz of voices. Then it turned into neighing, because suddenly I was in the stable, and Hero was gone... I ran across the fields calling his name over and over. Sometimes I thought I could hear him answer me from far away, but no matter how much I searched, I couldn't find him...

"The Night Riders must have taken him," yelled Vanessa and started laughing. "See, now he's neither yours nor mine. That's so much fairer, don't you think? It's no use looking for him. You'll never find him!"

When I woke up, it was early morning and daylight outside. The dream stayed with me, so I threw on some clothes and hurried outside and over to the stable. Of course, I didn't seriously believe that the Night Riders had been there, but what if Vanessa had... what if...?

Hero was standing in his stall, as clean and unharmed as when I left him, but his mood wasn't as good. He tossed his head and neighed agitatedly at me. I could see why, too. The horses on both sides of him had gotten their breakfast already, but not him.

"There you are, finally!" said Steven's voice behind me. "Would you please unlock that thing so that I can give that loudmouth of yours some food? I expect he's about ready to kick down the wall by now! You'd think he was starving to death! And what, may I ask, is the point of putting chains and a big padlock on his door?"

I turned to Steven. "I wanted to make sure nobody could take him outside for

any more rides in the middle of the night," I said triumphantly. "And it worked! Pretty smart, huh?"

"Totally crazy, that's what it is!" said Steven in a resigned tone of voice. "What if there had been a fire in the stable during the night? During a fire there's not a second to lose, and a horse that's locked up like this, with no key nearby..."

He didn't say any more. He didn't have to either. I felt as if my body was turning stiff. That thought hadn't occurred to me at all! I had been so determined to prevent anybody from sneaking off with Hero again.

Now I felt completely awful. I only wanted to help Hero, but instead I had put his life at risk!

"Relax! After all, nothing happened," said Steven when he saw the expression on my face. "And I can see now that you really are convinced that somebody else is riding your horse in the night, because otherwise you wouldn't have done this. I should have listened to Haley, and taken you more seriously. I'm sorry that I didn't do that, but truly, I thought you just... never mind what I thought... However, I can promise you one thing, we're going to find out what's going on around here..."

I felt a wave of relief at Steven's words, at knowing that he finally believed me. Maybe now he would help me see to it that nothing bad happened to my pony.

And maybe he would be able to catch Vanessa red-handed the next time she tried something, I thought optimistically as I watched Steven throw some hay into Hero's stall. Hero started chowing down the food with a ravenous appetite. The sight warmed my heart, and I stayed there, petting my pony while Steven continued his feeding round.

"Gee, Haley sure has gone out early today," he commented a moment later. "That's so unlike her. She's certainly not in the habit of being first in the stable."

As I was stood looking at Hero, safe and sound in his stall eating contentedly, a slight uneasiness started creeping down my spine. I tried to brush it off. Haley had probably woken up earlier than normal and felt like taking a quiet ride before breakfast. There was probably nothing wrong... surely not... but what if...

As if Steven had read my mind, he said, "I don't like this. I have a feeling that something's wrong. Would you do me a favor, and feed the rest of the horses while I run up to the house and check?"

He left without waiting for an answer. I hurried out of Hero's stall and went to get food for the remaining horses that hadn't had their breakfasts yet. They weren't hard to find. The impatient neighing they greeted me with said very clearly, "Would you hurry up and give me something to eat, please! We've waited long enough!"

I had just carried an armful of hay in to the last horse, when I heard rapid steps approaching. The door was flung open and there was Steven... and Haley!

"Is she back?" Haley almost yelled.

"Who?" I asked, stupidly, because I knew she was talking about Lotus. "No, your horse isn't here. We thought you'd gone for a ride..."

Haley shook her head. "I was on my way to breakfast when Steven ran in."

She ran over to the stall, as if she couldn't believe that Lotus was gone until she saw it for herself. When she turned toward us again, she looked like she was on the verge of tears.

"Somebody has stolen my horse!" she said. "We have to call the police!"

"Let's wait a minute before we do that." Steven stroked a hand across his forehead. "Lotus may not be stolen. Maybe some-body just took her for a ride..."

"This is all my fault!" I cried.

"Your fault?" Haley looked at me, astonished. "I don't understand... How can this be your fault? You didn't ride out on Lotus, did you?"

I shook my head. "No, of course not. But I locked up Hero, so that Vanessa couldn't take him, and now she's taken Lotus instead!"

"No way – I cannot believe that!" Steven burst out. "Vanessa wouldn't do something like that!"

"Yes, she would!" I glared angrily at Steven. "How many times do I have to say it? She's jealous because Hero is mine and not hers. She didn't like the fact that I got to ride Lotus, either. Anybody could see that! So when she couldn't get Hero last night, she took Lotus instead, just to be mean to me! Or maybe because she wanted to ride Lotus, but didn't dare to ask, or something..."

Uncertain, I fell silent as I noticed the skeptical looks on Steven's and Haley's faces.

"Fine, you don't have to believe me," I said. "Why don't you just go up to the house and check for yourselves? I'll bet anything that Vanessa isn't there!"

I turned on my heel and walked out of the stable with long, angry strides. I was fuming inside. Why wouldn't they believe me? I heard steps behind me, and knew that Steven and Haley had followed, but I didn't turn around.

At the house, people had started gathering for breakfast. I caught a glimpse of Chelsea just as I swept past the door and marched toward the stairs to the second floor. Vanessa wasn't with her.

Of course she wasn't, I thought, taking the steps two at a time. She was out there, riding Lotus. But how could she be so careless as to not come home before people started coming to the stable? That was strange. What if something happened?

I stopped outside Vanessa's room and turned around. Steven and Haley were right behind me. "Here, take a look for yourselves!" I said triumphantly and flung the door open. "She's not... What the... ?"

"Go away!" Vanessa lifted her head and threw a dead glance at us. "I'm so sick I think I'm going to die! I don't feel like talking to anybody."

Then she sank back down on the pillow and closed her eyes. Her being sick was beyond any doubt. Her face had a greenish paleness to it, and on the floor in front of her was a bucket that smelled of vomit.

I backed out into the hallway just as Brenda came up the stairs. "How's she doing?" she asked. "Poor thing, I've been checking on her all night. She's been really sick, but I think the worst is over now." Brenda went into Vanessa and closed the door without waiting for an answer. I don't think I could have answered her anyway. About a million confusing thoughts were bombarding my mind. At least that's how it felt. Vanessa was in her room! She wasn't riding Lotus out in the woods. She was sick, and not only that, Brenda said she had been sick all night. I had been so sure, so completely convinced that it was Vanessa.

And I was still sure that she had ridden Hero the night before – or hadn't she? Everything started spinning around me, and I had to lean on the wall.

"I don't get it – now I don't understand anything," I said numbly. "This doesn't make any sense at all!"

"Go into my office and wait there. I'm just going to check something."

Steven started downstairs. Haley and I followed slowly. Neither of us said anything. I saw Steven go into the dining room. Haley opened a door on the left at the bottom of the stairs and waved for me to come inside. We sat down to wait. That is, I sat down, while

Haley paced the floor and started biting her nails.

"Do you know what Steven is up to?" I finally asked.

"I assume he's checking if any of the campers are missing," said Haley. "I'll wait to call the police until he comes back."

Just then we heard a horse's neighing outside. Haley stormed outside, with me right at her heels.

"Lotus!" she shouted. "She's back!" Lotus was standing in the farmyard with the saddle on her back and the reins hanging between her forelegs. The beautiful horse was all sweaty and worked up.

Haley hurried over to her mare. "Oh, Lotus," she said. "Are you all right?"

Lotus couldn't answer that, of course, but she seemed fine as far as I could tell. Haley let her hands slide down one of the forelegs, then the other. Afterwards she checked the hind legs.

"She seems to be okay," she said, relieved.

"But where's the rider?" I asked, as if I expected Haley to know. "She must have had a rider, right?"

"Well, it looks like it," said Haley. "But who could it be?"

"Nobody at the riding camp, anyway," said Steven, who had shown up while Haley examined Lotus. "I did a roll call, and everybody except Vanessa is sitting inside eating breakfast."

"Is it possible that it could have been one of them anyway?" I suggested. "If one

of them rode her, and Lotus threw them off and ran away, then maybe whoever it was gave up finding her and came back here, acting as if nothing happened..."

At this point I ran out of air and had to stop to take a breath.

Steven and Haley looked at each other.

"I guess that's possible," said Steven after a while, "but..."

He was interrupted by Chelsea who came storming out of the house, with a wild look in her eyes. "Is it true that Lotus is back? Without a rider?"

Steven nodded. Then Chelsea started

crying. Now I understood even less than I had before. Was it possible that Chelsea was the one who had been out riding? I stared at her suspiciously, remembering the night I had stood by the window imagining that the Night Riders had come to get me. I hadn't been able to tell if there were one or two riders out there. Could it have been both Vanessa and Chelsea? I hadn't thought about that before. And then Chelsea had ridden out alone last night because Vanessa was sick...?

My thoughts were interrupted by Chelsea screaming desperately, "We have to look for her, right away! She might be injured, and lying somewhere. I told her she shouldn't do it, but she never listens to me! Why did she even have to come here? I should never have gone along with it and agreed to keep quiet about her stupid plan! Never!"

"What are you talking about? What plan? And who are we supposed to look for? All the campers are here!" Steven looked at Chelsea as if he thought she had lost it.

Before Chelsea could answer, we heard a scream from the other side of the house.

"What was that?" Steven took off, and Chelsea and I followed him. Haley stayed behind with Lotus.

I'll never forget the sight that met us as we rounded the corner of the house. Along the wall was a row of bushes. From behind these bushes crawled a familiar figure, whimpering and holding a hand to her shoulder.

"Chelsea?" I said stupidly. Because of course it wasn't Chelsea. Chelsea was standing right next to me. But aside from the fact that this girl was all dirty and had tangled hair, it could have been.

I stared at her with my mouth open while the truth slowly dawned on me. This had to be...

"Courtney!" said Chelsea. "What happened?"

"I tried to climb in the window. But I failed, along with my entire plan. Just because I fell off that stupid horse!"

Steven stared at the Chelsea copy as if he had seen a ghost.

"What's the matter? Haven't you seen identical twins before?" Courtney tossed her head with a stubborn look on her face.

"Are you... were you the one we...?"

Courtney nodded. "That's right, I'm the one whose vacation you destroyed! You gave my place to her!"

She pointed accusingly at me, as if it was all my fault. I cringed at the hostile look on her face.

"Oh, come off it, Courtney," said Chelsea, looking as if she was on the verge of tears. "It wasn't Shannon's fault, which you know perfectly well! You're being totally unfair, which I've been trying to tell you this whole time!"

I looked in disbelief from one to the other. The whole thing seemed completely unreal. When Chelsea told me how bossy Courtney was, I had just assumed that Courtney was her older sister. Chelsea hadn't mentioned that they were twins.

"Have you been here, both of you, the whole time?" Steven demanded to know.

Chelsea turned toward him. "No, Courtney showed up totally unexpected,. on the night Haley told that ghost story..."

"You said you'd argued with her on the phone!" I said, glaring at Chelsea. "But that was a lie, wasn't it?"

"It's true that I argued with her, but not on the phone. She was in my room when I got upstairs. I tried to tell her she had to go back home, but she wouldn't listen to me. She never listens to me..." Chelsea fell silent and looked at the ground.

Courtney shrugged her shoulders. "I deserved being at this camp too – the prize was just as much mine as yours! So

I lied to Dad and told him that a place had opened up for me after all. Steven had said that if somebody got sick and had to go home, then we could get their place. That's why Dad believed me and drove me here, even though Mom didn't want to. She was saying some nonsense about Chelsea needing a chance to be here without me..."

"And she was right," Chelsea uttered and started crying again. "I had a great time until you showed up. Now it's all ruined, and it's your fault!"

Courtney looked a little uneasy then. "I didn't mean to ruin it for you..."

She glanced furtively at Steven. "I figured that Chelsea and I could take turns at the riding lessons. I didn't expect it to be a problem since everybody thinks we look so much alike."

"I should never have said yes," sniffled Chelsea. "I should have known that it would only mean trouble. You always jump into things without thinking them through..."

"Not thinking? The first night I was here, thinking was all I did – and being bored out of my mind, while everyone else was drinking hot cocoa and having a great time. I had to wait until people had gone to bed before Chelsea could sneak down to the kitchen and get some food to bring upstairs for me..."

Courtney made a face. "That's when I realized that it wasn't going to be as much fun as I had thought to share the camp with Chelsea. I don't think I would have had a hard time convincing her to go home and leave her space to me, but I knew that our mom would go ballistic if I did, so I had to forget it. If I wanted to ride as much as possible, I had to find some other way... So I pumped Chelsea for information about everything and everybody at the camp, and found out who had taken my spot. Then she told me the story about the Night Riders. And that's when I got the idea of how I could get rid of Shannon and get my place back..."

Chapter 11

Peace At Last

It was afternoon, and I took Hero into the farmyard to groom him outside in the nice weather. I had just barely started when loud voices made me turn my head. It was Chelsea and Courtney's parents. They had come to pick up the twins and take them home, and it wasn't hard to tell that they were furious. They practically shoved the girls into the back seat, and then the car spun out of the yard faster than the speed of light. As I stood and watched them leave, I saw out of the corner of my eye somebody coming out of the stable. It was Haley, with Vanessa following behind.

I said "hi" to Haley, but pretended not to see Vanessa. I felt embarrassed and angry at the same time. Embarrassed because I had been wrong to accuse her of being the nighttime rider, and angry because of the things she had said and done to ruin the camp for me. My anger got the best of me. If she thought I was going to apologize for having suspected her, she'd better think again.

I started brushing Hero with such hard, fast strokes that he turned his head and looked surprised. "Hey, would you let me keep at least some of my coat?" he seemed to be thinking. I patted him on the flank and took it a little easier. Poor Hero, this wasn't his fault!

"Vanessa has something she wants to say to you," said Haley, giving Vanessa a light nudge in the back.

I glanced guardedly over at Vanessa. She didn't look as if she wanted to say anything. There was an awkward silence, but finally Vanessa cleared her throat and said, "I'm sorry I've been mean to you." She squirmed, clearly ill at ease. "– and for hiding the bridle in Hero's stall."

"Why did you do that?" I looked at her.

Vanessa shrugged her shoulders. "Chelsea gave me the idea. Or, I thought it was Chelsea, but I guess it must have been Courtney. It seemed like a good idea at the time. I was really mad at you for that thing with the rock. I thought of Hero,

that he could have gotten hurt because you didn't care enough to check his hooves. And I honestly thought that you blamed me just because you wanted to hide the fact that you hadn't taken care of him properly. At least I thought so at first... so I thought you deserved whatever trouble you got into! I had no idea that it was Courtney, and not you, who did those things to Hero."

"Courtney told me the whole story about her double act while we waited for her parents to come and pick up her and Chelsea," said Haley. "She took a long ride on Hero the first night, trying to come up with a way to get you to go home, Shannon. At first she planned on riding Hero so hard that he would start limping, but fortunately she came to her senses when she realized that she risked causing serious injury to the horse. That wasn't what she wanted. She claims she loves horses way too much to do that."

If she loves horses, she sure had a funny way of showing it! I shuddered at the thought of what could have happened to Hero while he was out riding with her.

"When she came back from the ride, she jammed a sharp stone underneath his hoof," continued Haley. She looked at me. "She was hoping that you wouldn't discover it until after Hero started limping. An injury like that wouldn't be too serious, but it would cause you to go home, she figured. But as we know, that wasn't what happened, and that's when she resorted to more drastic measures to get rid of you. She claimed that you deserved it, and that Vanessa agreed with her."

"I behaved like an idiot," said Vanessa. "I kept whining about how Shannon had practically stolen Hero from me. And Courtney lapped up every word I said. She probably figured that if Shannon had behaved so conniving toward me, then she didn't have to feel guilty about using whatever means necessary to get rid of Shannon as soon as possible."

Vanessa snuck a glance at me. "Truth be told, I knew perfectly well that you didn't steal Hero from me, but I was so angry and jealous that I wanted to believe the worst about you. I... I had this ridiculous dream that if everybody saw that you didn't

take proper care of him – and that is what I believed – then you'd have to give him up, and then he could become mine after all. Stupid, wasn't it?"

"I'd say so!" uttered Haley. "No wonder Shannon suspected you of being the Night Rider, the way you behaved!"

Vanessa shook her head without saying anything. She looked so miserable that I couldn't help feeling sorry for her.

I looked at her. "I said a lot of mean things to you too. But I honestly did believe that it was you who was riding Hero in the night! You have no idea how desperately I wanted you to be sent home!"

"But instead it was two others who had to go," Vanessa gave a slanted smile. "Oh, I was almost pulled out too. Steven was so mad at me for that stunt with the bridle that he wanted to send me straight home as well. Fortunately Haley managed to talk him out of it."

"I just thought you deserved a second chance," said Haley calmly. "That night when we talked, you weren't able to hide just how jealous and unhappy you were about Hero belonging to Shannon instead of you. You've done some stupid things, but you do love horses, and I couldn't believe you would actually do something to hurt Hero. In my eyes, there's a huge difference between the things you did and what Courtney was doing, with Chelsea's reluctant consent."

I pictured Chelsea's unhappy face and noticed a sinking feeling in my stomach. Poor Chelsea! Maybe I ought to feel angry with her for having allowed Courtney to do those things to me, but all I could feel was pity for her. With Courtney, it was a different story. Her, I would never forgive.

"Too bad Chelsea told Courtney the story about the Night Riders," said Haley. "If she hadn't, Courtney may not have come up with that crazy idea of riding Hero in the night. She said she thought it was kind of exciting and fun to play Night Rider, even though nobody believed in such a silly, old story anymore."

I felt my head getting warm. I had believed the story – at least... almost – but I was never going to admit it to anybody. That would be too embarrassing.

Vanessa shrugged her shoulders. "If so, she'd probably have come up with something else to make Shannon go home. She used me when she suggested that trick with the bridle, but I didn't see it then. I was too busy being jealous."

Haley also said that Chelsea had wanted to tell me the truth several times, because she felt so bad about it, but she just couldn't bring herself to tell on her own sister. She didn't dare to tell on her either, I thought to myself. Courtney didn't seem like somebody you would want to mess with. I was glad she wasn't my sister!

Hero gave a snort, and I stroked him across his soft muzzle. "No wonder I was confused by Chelsea's shifty moods," I said. "There were several times when I thought she was like two different people, but it never occurred to me that she actually was just that."

"Same here," said Vanessa. "They must have told each other pretty much every detail about things that happened during the day, so they never gave themselves away. Not until Courtney made the mistake of riding Lotus when she couldn't get hold of Hero."

"That was apparently supposed to be the last straw that would make Steven send you home for sure," said Haley and shook her head in resignation. "Chelsea said that Courtney had found a barrette that belonged to you. She planned to put it in Lotus's stall so that I would find it when I found my horse all dirty and sweaty. The barrette was supposed to "prove" that you were the one who had ridden her. But then she wasn't able to handle Lotus. She must have thought that since you had ridden her, Lotus would be easy to handle."

"She forgot the fact that I only rode her in the arena with you there to help me the whole time," I said.

"It's a good thing Lotus didn't get hurt. I don't know what I would have done to Courtney if that had happened!" Haley

made a face. "I don't even want to think about it. But fortunately everything ended well, both for Lotus and Hero."

Vanessa took a step closer to Hero and put a hand on his back.

"I'm still jealous, just so you know!" She looked at me. "But you didn't know

that I was planning to buy him. You see, I imagined that you had been told about it when you came to see him, and that you just didn't care. I understand now that it wasn't like that at all."

"I tried to tell you," I said. "But you wouldn't listen. Hero was a gift from my mom and grandma. They had been saving up money for a long time to buy him, just as you did. He's the best gift I ever got, and I love him very, very much!"

"I'm sorry I've been so foolish," said Vanessa. "And I promise that I won't be mean to you anymore... or maybe just a little bit, so you won't go into withdrawal..."

She smiled mischievously, and then we both started laughing. A little later, when I was riding Hero and waiting for the lesson to start, I felt incredibly happy and relieved. These past days had been difficult, but also educational in a way. And Vanessa and I would hardly be best friends ever, but it didn't matter. We had cleared the air between us, and I felt confident that the remaining days at the camp would be every bit as wonderful as I had hoped when I read the brochure back home and dreamed of getting to ride with Haley, my big idol...

Thanks to Sophie, Kristin, Julia, Hannah, and Mark, for
being the best models we could wish for.
Thanks to Tina, for all the help.
Thanks to all at Ludwigshof Riding Center in Speyer, for
letting us use the beautiful premises and the horses.